Last Calls

and

Lucky Charms

A Love Triangle

By Edward Sandison

Table of Contents

I must acknowledge a few—all will make sense as
you read.

Dedicated to all those emotionally unavailable
women out there.

In the liquor store, the office, the record store,
coworker and the school chum.

Thank you EMT Miranda Wickert for explaining the
legality and function of the job.

Thank you Renae, for the last scene, your love story is
a real one.

And thank you to my parents, married forty-five
years—who got engaged in 48 hours

The World called them crazy. They knew what you
were doing.

Thank you to my oldest daughter:

Love trumps blood.

Also to the Statesman Joe Arcudi, of Westport CT
who was what all leaders should be.

Thank you Mr. Decker for making me a writer.

Prologue
The Triangle

Matthew Jason Benson is a thirty-two year-old EMT, big and dreamily handsome. With his cleft chine and broad shoulders; he looks like a young Robert Vaughn. He is honest, loyal, hard-working and devout. He'd give you the shirt off his back if you asked. He is lonely though, no one has ever fallen in love with him. Someday, he dreams, a woman will say those three little words to him.

Horatio Albert Urban is buried under rejection slips. He can't remember what it feels like to be sober because he's too afraid not to drink. There was a time his eyes were bright and his typewriter lively but he can't remember it. Hal is twenty-eight, small and pasty and is lost. He got a job reporting sports scores accidently and is coasting. When it comes to theater and writing there is a genius hidden in there. He is a friend a friend would like to have.

Justine Anabeth Ducane is a thirty-year old tall chestnut haired beauty who never wears makeup and doesn't dress to impress. There is an unhealed emotional wound in there. She has given up on dating and pursuing a career in the politics she studied in college. The only conservative woman at a liberal paper she writes an angry column under a pen name. Justine also wears a fake engagement ring to scare the jerks away.

PART ONE
A Week in Spring, 1988

All the Words have gone away

The Pages are empty

The pen is dry

There is nothing left to say

Rejections have killed the writer

All the Words have gone away

I

TUESDAY

"Happy birthday to me," Justine Anabeth Duchane told her reflection. She stood in front of the bathroom mirror. The face staring back was looking more and more like her mother's every day. The hair was being brushed back in a ponytail, her mom preferred the chestnut hair down. There was no gray yet. She was also trying hard not to feel old. Night after night of counting cracks on the ceiling or watching talk shows, reruns and infomercials were taking their toll, however. It had also gotten her some great, dusty, exercise equipment.

So this was thirty. Where had her life gone? Justine had a masters in poli sci from URose. She had planned on…she couldn't remember anymore. Now she just wrote a column for the Rose Times. *The Decline of the American Empire: How Liberals Are Destroying America.* Writing in Connecticut she used a pen name. If anyone cares she was in decent shape and tall for her gender, five foot ten inches.

Duchane never painted her fingernails or wore makeup. For a long time, her attitude to all that was *Screw it.* Her pony tail that landed between her shoulders. The fact that she bothered to shave her legs and armpits anymore was a mystery to her. Men were intimidated by the only republican woman at a liberal paper and her life didn't lend itself to dating. She also wore a fake engagement ring to keep the assholes away.

The columnist went into the bedroom and opened a drawer of the oak dresser. Her room was the beige color it had been when she'd rented the townhome. On went a pair of granny panties and off went the towel. Then a matching teal bra. On went a nice pair of slacks and solid green turtleneck. On her dresser was picture of her family after high school graduation. There was deodorant, which she put on before tucking her shirt. No perfume to be found, none needed. There was a painting of a John Adams' inauguration on the opposite wall, next to her closet.

Over the bed was a framed picture of the Washington memorial. American politics were her true religion. The bed was a full. It had been bought by her parents. The sheets were gray and comforter as well. The towel was picked up off the bed and tossed in the hamper in her clean bathroom, then she killed the light. The most feminine thing about Justine Anabeth Duchane was her toes. No one saw them. She sat on the foot of the bed and pulled on black flats. The otherwise unadorned bedroom's light was flicked off as well.

Everything in the rest of the apartment was neat and clean and nothing was out of place. You'd think she dusted and vacuumed every day. Justine had had breakfast already. She went through the small living room to the front door. That light had never been turned on, sunlight and all. The front door was locked and she started her blue, 1985 Volkswagen Jetta. *Only fourteen more payments and it's mine.* There was traffic in the radio forecast. "Damn.

II

Horatio Albert 'Hal' Urban was awoken by the phone. He knocked a good bottle of Jack Daniels over reaching for the phone on the messy coffee table. The clock over the TV was fuzzy but he saw it well enough. "Shit." He pressed the button on the boxy portable phone. "Yup."

A velvety voice that made women swoon called to him. "Hal, are you sleeping?" The voice was that of the best friend a guy could have, Book Booker. He was the self-styled heir to Billy Dee.

"Not anymore." He sat up in his soiled yesterday's clothes. That was a mistake. "Ow." There was a caveman smashing rocks in his head.

"A little late even for you," Hal got up. He'd been through this before and stumbled to the kitchen. His little apartment living room was not much but it was messy. One secondhand chair one couch and one TV stand. There was a desk behind the couch facing the wall. The walls were decorated with uneven sports memorabilia of baseball, basketball and high school football. Yankees, Mets, Rose Thorns--the high school teams; you get the idea. There was more than a few empty pizza boxes and Chinese food containers.

The kitchen wasn't much better. "I see my column on the desk." Handwritten and full of errors. *What the hell?* It was Tuesday. They went to press that night not in the morning.

He pressed the button on the coffee machine and went back through the living room to the open bedroom door. ESPN was still on the TV. He ignored it.

"Monica is gunning for you." *Great. Shit.*

"Can you stall her another half an hour?" She was their sports editor.

Why? He didn't really know. She knew nothing about sports. She wore tight mini skirts and dresses every day, she was a man eating woman in her forties with a Marilyn Monroe look, hair and all. She had the body to match and loved watching her employees squirm.

Ah, sexual harassment. The days before Clarence Thomas and Bill Clinton. All in all, Oberon Community Newspapers were a terrible place to work.

"Yeah, I got this. Next round's on you," that usually was the way it was with them. Again, the term 'enabler,' hadn't been coined yet.

"Love you brother." Click. Slowly and painfully the writer looked for his clean clothes of the mess in his little bedroom. He tossed the phone on his twin bed with Yankees sheets. They had been a gift. The dresser was almost as old as he was. There was a bathroom off one side of bedroom and a closet on the other side of the bed. Over the bed was an autographed Mr. October Poster. He pulled on cleanish khakis and a dress shirt.

The coffee mug was a Mets one from one promotion or another and Hal guzzled the hot liquid as he pulled his socks on and tied his shoes. He drank a second cup in front of ESPN taking notes on a notepad from his desk and then, trying to balance the mug on his knee it spilled--on his groin. Horatio Albert

Urban screamed a deafening scream and ran around in circles for a minute, almost tripping on the crap in his living room. He then ran into the bedroom and yanked his shoes off, looking for clean underwear and new pants. He pulled the pants from the hamper.

Well, at least he was awake. "Why did I drink this time?" He also wondered when he'd actually do laundry. Urban hesitated at the desk. There was an envelope he hadn't opened the night before. It was a *very* delayed letter. He opened it. After reading it he put it in the bottom drawer and went to door leaving his coffee mug on the couch.

The letter had been his 1027th rejection slip, albeit a year late. A novel, poems, short stories and plays--mostly plays. The sportswriter had tried it all. Not one thing published since college and that was in a school journal. Hell, he only got this job because of a letter to the editor and he hated it, he hated every minute of it.

"Keys?" He looked at the TV. They were on the cable box. "Thank Buddha for small favors." The writer locked the door of his crappy apartment and the sun almost blinded him. The clock was not his friend, however. "Damn."

He was on the second floor of an exterior entrance u shaped living community. There was a rusting railing that had once been faux ornate. There was a trashed pool in the middle. It was empty. The last door he had to pass before the paint chipped stairs opened. *Doubledee damn.* A large fat Hindu, barefoot in jeans and a wife beater t shirt came out. He was an imposing sight. "Hal, my lad." The landlord had been British educated.

"Arty." The rent had been paid...right? The writer thought back. *Yeah, it had.*

"Late night? Later morning?" *Shit.*

"No," he lied.

"Oh, really?" Had he screamed that loud? *Shit.*

"Did I scream loudly…?"Arty put a paw on Hal's shoulder. "Look, there was coffee and I spilled it and…"

"Horatio," the Hindu softened the 'a' for effect HOR-ahhh-tio, "my dear wife Sifa has been dead these two long years." The tenant looked at his shoes.

"I'm sorry," his buck sixty-five felt really small. The fat man laughed.

"I'm not. I date sexy Asian now. She's a lawyer." Arty belly laughed "Having money is wonderful. Vishnu bless America." *What?* "The point is that Sifa probably heard you scream in her grave and almost woke up." The verbal pressure was deadly. "Now, we wouldn't want that?"

"I, I,"--for a writer he had few words. "I think I get it."

"So no more screaming and we will all be happy, agreed?" At least the rent had been paid. *Better late than never.*

"Right." The landlord released him.

"Good." Arty patted his back. "Now, go." The big man returned to his apartment and shut the door. There was a click.

Hal walked down the stairs. He passed the elderly Mrs. Laponsee in her shawl and gray dress sleeping as if she was sunning by the empty pool. She had been sitting there for twenty years and the pool had been empty most of that time. It made the widow happy, her husband had swam in it.

At the bike rack the writer unlocked three locks and opened the chain. His car was in the shop, again-- and he didn't know when he would have the money to rescue it.

III

The beefy EMT benched Hal's weight.

Nothing personal, he didn't know Urban. Matthew Jason Belson was thirty-two and resembled a young Robert Vaughn, *Man From Uncle* years. He was in the weight room of the River Street in Cannonville Fire Department lifting weights and waiting for a call. The ambulance was downstairs and ready. Twenty-four on and twenty-four off, just like a fireman.

His shirt was soaked and he had just paused when Pamela Suzzette Tyler, his driving partner, a twenty-three-year old junior EMT came in with a video. She had long black hair in a bun. "You go to Pennyless Video?" It was down the street.

"I got *Platoon*, I've never seen it." He laughed. How young she was.

I'll be just a few minutes, okay?" She grinned. *Good girl.* "There's an envelope for you on the TV." His grandfather had collected stamps and so did Pam.

"The stamps!" She was giddy. "Thank you."

"Go enjoy them." Odd collection for her generation of women, but whatever. He didn't watch her go. Matt had one more set of twelve than a quick shower.

The seasoned EMT had never cheated on a girl, never got a traffic ticket and was never late for work. He had a six pack and a chin dimple. If he saved himself for marriage, great.

It was Tuesday. Matt hadn't been on a 911 call in two shifts and was feeling useless, he also was grateful no one was hurting on his shift. He was a devout man who had worked his way through UROSE on ambulances and then stayed on.

In a couple years he may be promoted and the EMT thing would officially be a career. He was a catch for any woman. Nobody's perfect? Or are they?

IV

Monica Shafer wore a short red dress, red heels and swayed her hips. All the men noticed, especially the ones that answered to her. That's what she counted on. She was mercenary with her sexuality. She stood five six, but always had four inch heels on, to look down at everyone. With her soft blue eyes and high cheekbones. Contrary to the way she made men squirm, she was in a happy monogamous marriage to the News editor, Pete Shafer. It was about power. She had it.

"Urban," he looked up from his desk that was as sloppy as the slob he was, forgive the alliteration. He was scared. That's what the boss counted on. "I can see why you should be writing fiction," she dropped Monday's column on the desk. Book's desk was back to back and he listened without letting on. There was more red ink than black ink on the two pages. *Shit.*

"I-I wil," came the sheepish response, "s-someday,"--*silly pipedream.*

It did not placate the angry boss. "That's great, but don't start with your sport's commentary. "*Dan* Mattingly has never won an MVP."

Hal picked up the copy. "Whoops." *Don* Mattingly.

"Whoops' is right. Another thing, I'm sick to death of baseball and it's only a cold day in April. Find me something new!" He was getting around to something else.

"Of course Mon, no problem," she wasn't listening.

"Am I Professor Shafer? Am I your high school English teacher?" Oh she was on a roll. Even Booker had to grin.

The writer swallowed. "Um, no ma'am."

"Then no more messing around Hal," the spat order was deafening to the hungover brain. She leaned over his desk which made him more squirmy. He about crapped his pants. "Get this rewritten, flawlessly edited in thirty minutes." She stood up.

"Absolutely," but he was speaking to her disappearing hips. Her office was about thirty feet away. Hal pulled the paper out of typewriter and put in a blank sheet.

"Don't mind the boss," Book turned around and came close to his friend. He wore a nice silk black suit, black shirt and black tie. Yep, Bertram B. Booker always looked good. "Scuttlebutt is that she and Pete had a fight."

"Oh?" Hal laughed. "Serpent in Eden?"

"Can you finish all this crap by six?" The writer checked his Star Trek clock.

"Um, I guess, why?" *Cause I owe him a round, stupid!*

"Come shoot darts with me," seeing how early it was and as long as Monica didn't get her panties in a bunch any more it was likely he'd make it.

"Promise not to gamble on it?" Hal never won. His vision was fuzzy after a few.

Book crossed his heart. "I swear I won't take your money." They laughed and the smaller man's demeanor lightened. Book was always good for that.

"Leave me alone so I can work and I'll be there." Booker patted his back.

"You're a peach." He turned back to his desk.

Another error! "Damn." He reached for another blank sheet. None. "Damn." He stood up.

"Get me a ream while you're in there, good buddy." Yeah, it was his turn and Book wasn't stupid. The pasty little sportswriter stood.

"Right." Hal stretched. "No paper. No words and no paper. No words on no paper. No words!" He got excited.

"What?" Booker asked.

"I think I got a sonnet," Hal grabbed a pen and small spiral pad and began to write as he walked. "All the words that I had to say have been said," and he went down the aisle of Monica's army of sportswriters towards the hall where the copy room was. "All the tales have told...oh that's good."

"What's good?" Another writer, Chuck or Chad asked.

"I think I have a sonnet," Hal repeated and kept writing while walking, bad idea. The other man disappeared. Coming out of the copy room Justine was reading her pen name's tenth death threat of the day, ream under her arm, she didn't look up either.

All the Words have gone away

The Pages are empty

The pen is dry

There is nothing left to say

Rejections have killed the writer

All the Words have gone away

"Oh you are sick," she laughed. "Liberals." The letter writer had complimented her by comparing her Margaret Thatcher and her writing to Peggy Noonan's, Reagan's speechwriter.

So needless to say, neither Duchane nor Urban were paying attention. She walked right into the scrawny writer. Pad, envelope, ream, pen and letter went flying and they wound up on their butts. The two co-workers looked at each other embarrassed. They finally started to get up. "I'm so sorry," Hal begged forgiveness. He picked up her letter and the envelope. "Are you alright?" He felt ashamed. So did she.

"I think *I* should have been looking where *I* was going, I'm fine. Are you?" The political commentator picked up his pad and pen. "I think this is yours."

"And this is,"--he stopped when he realized Justine was reading his sonnet.

"Did you write this?" she asked, holding it out. She studied the writer's exhausted face. The unmade up face almost smiled at him.

"Erm...yes." They traded and she got her ream. They let some co-workers pass by.

"You wrote this walking from the sports desk to here?" They traded looks and then Hal looked at his drivel, quite ashamed.

"Yeah, I know it's not very good,"--Justine cut him off.

"No it's really good." A half-hearted smile appeared on our heroine's face. No one ever saw her smile. They straightened up.

"More like the job feeds writer's block." He thought of the three, almost four years he'd worked there. It was hell. "Hmmm. Feeds writer's block...I should save that." He wrote it down.

Justine almost smirked. "Don't give up." *Cause I listened to that so well.*

Hal shrugged. "I'll get a story published when you get elected."

"*Touché.* Is that the office rumor? I'm so political I need to be elected somewhere?" He was right. She'd like that.

"Nah. Your pal Kelli dated," that was a strong word for it, "my friend Book for a while. It came up one day at the bar. She called you a future governor." *In my dreams maybe.*

"Well, keep writing like that and you've got a better shot at being a published writer," Justine turned and went.

"And...," she heard behind her.

Justine took the left to her cubicle. Unfortunately, as there were only two political columnists at a really big Oberon Community Newspapers, they sat where there was room--on opposite sides of the building. She barely knew the liberal one, Celine Bohner, who sat on the far side of the other paper published out of that office, the Cannonville News. The building was actually in Cannonville, not Rose. One Rose City daily, one Cannonville town biweekly.

More unfortunately was that when the previous owner, Vladimir Oberon hired her the only space personnel could find was right outside his major office. Though it was annoying under Oberon, when his nephew took over, upon Vlad's massive coronary, it got worse. Mac was an oversexed overgrown child who wanted her bad and she detested him.

The political columnist grabbed a pen a post it and wrote a note. 'Friday's column, Liberal Death Threats.' That made her laugh. "It's an idea."

"I saw a bumper sticker today for Dukakis," a voice came from the other hall. *Damn.* "Maybe you should make that a column." A powerful over scented frame leaned on her desk.

She looked at the man who signed her checks. "Never happen." He laughed. Behind him was his outer office, one desk on the left where Lenor, the matronly administrative assistant he had inherited with the paper who really did all the work and on the right two smaller desks where the twin 'secretaries,' Yvette and Brianna did their makeup and nails respectively. They weren't there for their typing skills. Mac was a man of passions, like Uncle 'Bad Vlad' Oberon. Beyond the ladies was a closed frosted glass door with Mac's full name on it: Theodore Roosevelt Maguire Jr. He was a powerfully built man who made forty look like thirty.

"Whatever. I don't want you calling him 'socialist' anymore. It's too harsh." She cackled. "Why can't you steer clear of this jingoistic crap?"

"Well, you say not to tell the truth, but every time I've done that for five years it has created word of mouth and boosted sales for both of your papers. That's why your uncle hired me," Justine snapped back, completely unafraid.

"You leave my uncle out of this!" he recoiled at the phrase. They might have the same passions and same sins but Vladimir Oberon knew how to sell papers, Theodore Roosevelt Maguire did not.

"I will not." She stood up to her full height. Not his six foot two but she made him feel small. "*He* hired me. *He* signed my contract. An iron clad contract to protect me and my one clear voice from your bullshit because my column is honest, factual and sells papers." *Mental note, name tomorrow's column One Clear Voice.*

"One year, three months and seven days I can fire your ass for insubordination." Mac rattled off the number like Rain Man. If he ever used his Harvard education that would really be something.

"Keep making reference to my buttocks and I'll sue your ass for sexual harassment so fast that those two trollops behind you will have whiplash.

"If she doesn't, I will." In a gray pantsuit Lenor stood in the doorway with her short gray haired sixty-year-old head. She had her arms crossed. The older woman stepped aside and gestured for him to retreat to his office.

"Bitch," Mac hissed and too angry to speak he trudged past the older woman and slammed his inner office door. There was the sound of applause from the general direction of the lady's room.

The columnist's friend Kelli appeared from there. A bit chunky, blonde and freckled and in a full green dress with matching open toed shoes. Justine sat and put her feet on her desk, leaning back on her hands. "Well said." She looked at her bubbly friend and nodded.

"A bit, I've ripped him better." Kelli and Lenor laughed.

"Keep wearing that engagement ring and every man in this office will be afraid of you, not just him," Her friend went on. That ruffled Justine's feathers but her friend was right. It was better to be ignored than feared.

"He still thinks you're taken," Lenor argued. "Most men here do."

"I need to write," she opened the ream. "Lots of column."

"And more ammo," the blonde picked up a mail bag from in front of the desk. "An entire bag of letters address to your *non de pleur.*

"Damn." The older woman went back to work.

Kelli put the bag down. "Price of fame pal."

Justine ignored her and typed 'One Clear Voice.'

V

One half mile north of the fire station where Benson parked his ambulance, still on River Street was the intersection with Wappinger Avenue. On that corner was Oberon Community Newspapers and three doors down was two story up two story down parking lot and then a bar and grill called TC Referees. Across the street was a strip mall and public parking. There was a small alley in between the public parking lot and the office building. Hal's bike was locked up at the office and Justine's car was in the garage.

It was after sunset, street lights on. The same moment Hal left the bar after a few rounds and three games of darts Justine left the office to walk to her car.

"Damn bike," but the writer's speech was already slurred. He'd be safer biking back to Rose.

Justine barely noticed him in the distance when she heard a voice from the shadowy alley. "Honey." It was creepy and she tried to ignore it but a powerful hand grabbed her wrist and dragged her into the shadows past a dumpster and metal garbage cans.

"What the,"--she could barely see the white attacker under his ripped ski mask--so clique, matted long hair, muddy boots, old jeans and fully buttoned canvas shirt.

"Behind the dumpster bitch." She did see the knife.

Aw fuck it. "Fire!"

"Shut up!" The attacker slapped her.

"Fire!" She screamed again and one scrawny writer came running down the alley. Not exactly Harrison Ford, but he'd have to do. "Fire!"

"Who is it?" He recognized Justine. "Oh my God." He came around the dumpster.

The attacker whirled to the oncoming...gentle breeze. Come on, Mike Tyson Hal wasn't. He was just a nice guy trying to help. The bigger man waved the knife and then kicked Urban in the groin, sending him backwards head first into the brick wall. Urban crumpled to the ground.

"Fuck you!" Justine clocked the attacker cold with the metal lid of a garbage can, the stranger went down hard and she kicked the knife away. "Hal."

"Oh, daddy my head." He was barely conscious, Johnnie Walker Black hadn't helped.

"Come on Rambo." She pulled him to his feet and put an arm under his shoulders getting his over hers. "To the street lights Robin."

Very deliberately, as fast as her would be rescuer could manage *ugh the breath* Duchane led him out of the alley. "Justine?"

"Yes, Terminator?" she asked sarcastically. The joking took her mind off what had nearly happened. It was scary even for the toughest woman.

"You hate me," left towards the crowd coming out of TC Referees.

"Don't flatter yourself." Apparently someone had called 911, they heard sirens. "That would require me thinking about you on a regular basis."

Book Booker and a Latina that Justine did not recognize came rushing up to them. "Hal?" Book accepted his friend's weight.

"Some guy attacked me in the alley, your pal here…if he hadn't taken the hit for me…" she let them fill in the blanks.

"Betram?" Horatio Albert Urban mumbled at his friend, who saw the blood in his hair.

"Shhh," he gestured to his date, "Romeo."

"Wrong play Rosencrantz," the bigger man smiled.

"There you go, you'll be fine." Roz, the lady with Book, in her tight jeans, low cut white top and hoop earrings, handed Booker some tissues from her purse which he applied it to his friend's head. She was buxom and slutty, the way the ebony Adonis liked them.

The sirens were coming closer. There was a groan in the alley. "How many?" Roz asked.

"Just one." Hal was getting lucid.

"He can't be that stupid," Book began, but two blue and whites parked in front of them before the attacker appeared from the alley.

A redheaded female cop got out of one car, gun drawn and pointed it down the alley. "On your knees." She seemed to recognize him. Two male cops, younger, moved slower. "Pull the mask, it's our guy." She had the air of earned authority. A fourth cop, younger and female, came up to Hal and Justine.

"Are you alright?" She asked. An ambulance pulled up.

"I am, but Rambo here got hit trying to save me," the political theorist gestured. Two EMTS, one big and male and one small and female approached with their tool chests. I like calling them EMT bags, but I always get yelled at.

The male cops had the attacker handcuffed, he looked like an Aryan poster boy. The captain holstered her weapon and joined them. One EMT, Tyler, as her name tag said, went to Hal, shining a little light in his eyes. "Blankets Matt," the captain called to the other EMT, his nametag read Benson. He put the bag down and ran back.

When the cop was close enough Justine read the name tag. Sullivan-Hastings. She knew it well. Conservative female cop. Smart and accomplished. "You know him captain?"

"The EMT?" she laughed. "Good at his job."

"No, him," Duchane pointed in the back of the blue and white.

"He's been arrested twice, hasn't stuck. We've been after his tail three months. I think this time it will stick." She wore no makeup and her uniform was loose-she was also a decade or more older--but she made Roz and Justine feel plain.

"Okay, let's sit Hal on the car," Pam told Book, who nodded. They led him to the other police car's hood. "I'll take it from here." She had gloves on and replaced the tissues with gauze, examining the area. "He'll need stitches."

Benson handed Book a blanket who draped it over his friend and then Matt looked at Justine. Who looked at him. He hesitated. Captain Sullivan-Hastings was continuing. "Will you give a statement?" that brought the political theorist back from Matt's dreamy brown eyes.

Though her face was now on his mind now. *Shit.* Bad timing.

"Uh," she looked at the cop. "Of course." He offered her the blanket. She shook her head. "I'm fine. Thanks anyway." He nodded and put it next to Hal, watching his partner work.

"Can we move him?" he asked his partner. She just nodded.

"I'll help." Book gave Pam the smolder, she ignored him. He wasn't exactly her type. Neither was Matt. Don't ask, don't tell.

"Can you walk sir?" Hal smirked.

"Sure, doctor." He was clearly inebriated.

"Okay, okay. Hold the gauze Pam, let us use our upper body strength." She gave him a dead arm with her free hand--and without looking up, "you can't hit your partner." Tyler smirked. Booker and Benson got the sort of hero up.

As he got into the ambulance the small sportswriter could have sworn that heard Justine say "he saved me." That made him smile.

"I'll be right back," Benson went back. Other than a small contusion on her wrist that he inspected quickly as Duchane spoke to the police captain she seemed uninjured. She almost let herself smile.

"I'm fine." He nodded at her and then at the captain.

"He'll need stitches." She nodded back.

"Get him to Saint M.'s," hospital, "keep me posted." She shook his hand.

"Ma'am." He smiled at Justine and picked up both bags and the blanket. Roz had joined Book at the ambulance.

"Saint M's?" Book asked.

"Yes." Pam told him.

"I'll drop Roz off and meet you there good buddy." He patted Hal's shoulder and exited. The EMT got Urban into a good position on the gurney. "And you did good tonight." He walked away, holding his date's hand.

Justine was still talking to the policewoman as the ambulance doors closed.

VI

Mac was alone, at home, watching porn on his immense empty bed--sweat soiling silk sheets when the phone rang. "Maguire," he paused the VCR.

"Mac, It's Sully." Captain Sarah Sullivan Hastings, CPD. He hated her. Mostly because he couldn't seduce her. Couldn't seduce her in high school either. *Damn that outfielder*. Maguire had been a great athlete at Saint. M's high school. A great pitcher! Not friends with the team though. Not friends with anyone.

"What do you want, *Sarah*?" She ignored him. *No* one called her that.

"Two of your employees were involved in an altercation…" He smiled.

"Sounds like I can spin this as a hero story." She sighed.

"Just pay his hospital bill." That's why she called?

"What?" Oberon Community Newspapers did offer crummy insurance.

"That young man is a hero. He saved another employee from a rapist. You do the right thing." She hung up the phone.

Mac stood up and started to think of the headline. "HERO SPORTSWRITER," but the editor looked at the TV and felt disgusted.

That young man is a hero.

Hero.

Those women...He punched the TV, shattering it and skinning his knuckles. "This is not living." The big editor was disgusted with himself. "No!"

His hand hurt and he needed a new television but Mac felt better.

After getting some gauze she called the owner of the Rose Hour, his principal rival. "This better be good." It was a new day.

WEDNESDAY

Dr. Elizabeth Victoria Burma had decided to make one patient her personal issue. When Matt and Pam had wheeled him in he was lucid and just needed a few stitches but she kept him overnight and did blood work anyway. She had never had children and was not yet forty but felt very maternal sometimes. She and her husband loved children. Since her shift ended after her husband left for work she just got another cup of coffee and looked at the lab results.

Hal looked familiar. That made her more worried so she called her favorite little sister. Okay. I'm her only little sister. I was twenty-nine at the time, ten years her junior. "Ellis, it's me," she began.

"What's wrong?" I asked her. Oh, my name is Alice Marie Bennett, call me Ellis or leave me alone. I worked at Pennyless Video and I went to night school.

Liz's office was not big nor was it impeccable. Medical journals and envelopes were not sorted and at least one the three unmoving chairs was piled high. Hers was a rolling chair. There were file cabinets and one whole wall was a bulletin board filled with thank you cards from patients, some had pictures. There were medical awards on surfaces and shelves and diplomas obviously. Her wedding photo was on the wall next to a photo of her and me. Finally, a picture of us before dad died with him and one of just him. There was not one of mom, I never asked her 'why not?'

"Do you know someone named Horatio Albert Urban?" I thought for a long time. No Hipaa in 1988.

"Yeah. We went to Saint M's high school together. Scholarship kid...he was a bookworm." I thought back...I had been smoking pot back then, it was hazy. "He was a budding writer. We took Journalism together. He did much better than me." She knew my grades. "Rents at the store once in a blue moon, usually when I'm not there."

"What kind of writer?" I laughed.

"You expect me to remember?" She waited.

"Yes, Ellis, I do." We laughed together.

"Oh yeah. He wrote a play and won an award...that's all I remember." I looked at the clock. "I gotta get to work."

"Thanks, love you." I had already hung up. Liz looked at the lab results again. Then she went to his room with a legal pad and pen. He was drinking water and nibbling toast.

Hal was sitting up in bed and watching the sports news. His doctor reached up and turned the TV off. "Hey."

"Let's talk." She sat and demurely crossed her legs.

"Um, am I going home today?" He waited for a response putting the toast down.

"I'm Dr. Burma, Attending Physician. I'm *your* doctor." She studied his exhausted face, curious. He didn't reveal anything.

"Hal." the patient shrugged. "You knew that."

"Don't worry, you'll be home soon." She paused. "I hear you're a writer."

"Sportswriter for Oberon Community Newspapers," neither were impressed.

"That's not the kind of writing I meant." This doctor, though younger, reminded him of his mom. Maternal and chiding.

"Well, a long time ago I dreamed of writing plays," Urban admitted. "Why?"

"You knew my sister Ellis in high school. She said you were a budding writer back then." He thought for a spell and laughed, his head made him wince.

"Yeah well, no offense to your sister, we didn't exactly travel in the same circles." Yeah, I was a stoner and he was an egghead.

"You were a great writer once. What happened?" That made the patient chuckle. But he stopped chuckling and frowned before he spoke.

"I don't know." The medicine lady shook her head.

"Yes you do." She pulled a prescription pad from her lab coat and waited. "When was the last time you went a week without a drink?"

"I'm not an alcoholic." Liz leaned forward and grabbed his chart, "too many rejections."

She began reading some things out loud. "Alcohol level…"

The room was blah. A double room, the other bed empty, privacy curtains open. Crucifix on the wall, it was a Catholic hospital. One window next to the closed bathroom door. A couple cabinets. Gray walls. There was a phone next to each bed. Those stupid rolling tables and two hospital beds. We all know what they looked like, even in 1988.

"Are you saying I need to go AA?" Hal was aghast.

"That would be your decision, but I will say I'm more worried about the alcohol content of your blood, your liver and worse, your broken dreams." The writer didn't buy it.

"I had a concussion and you're talking about broken dreams." Liz nodded. "How could that be worse?" Hal was confused.

"I stitched up your head last night and I will take those stitches out in eight weeks I want to see a full play written and your eyes clear of alcohol." She handed him the prescription which read that and the pad and pen. "Do you follow?"

"Insurance won't cover coming back to the hospital to get the stitches out," the sports writer was trying to weasel out.

"If you soberly bring a play, I won't charge you," the doctor smiled. "Maybe you can dedicate the play to me." He laughed.

She stood up and turned the TV back on. There was a baseball headline about a misconduct suspension. "If you are going play the game play it right, play it with respect." The medicine lady raised her eyebrows and studied her patient's face.

"That's a good start. Write that down. I'll see you soon." He began to write.

VII

Matt and Pam's shift was ending at noon. They were testing the blood pressure cuffs on each other. "Use the big boy cuff." He was thinking of the girl from last night.

"Where are you bud?" Tyler wasn't dumb.

"Oh Pam, I dunno."

"You had that stupid look on your face last night too," she reminded him. "Especially in front of that lady reporter.

"What?" He tried to scoff but Matt was transparent.

"Yeah, remember? We patched up the doofus that tried to play hero, you made an ass of yourself because of a pretty face." That was out of character for her partner.

"What was her name?" He asked her.

"Justine Duchane, Oberon Community Newspapers. Couldn't be easier lover boy." She undid the cuff. "You like her."

He looked away and almost blushed. "I couldn't."

"No reason you can't ask her out. No law against it." Not in 1988.

"No…"

"Go for it. Our shift's over anyway." He hesitated and then nodded. They bumped knuckles and parted company. Matt went to the men's locker room and Pam to the women's. In jeans, URose sweater and sneakers he walked up River Street. He stopped at the Mobil and got a terrible bouquet of flowers. The sign was almost the size of the building and was also in different fonts, *interesting*:

OBERON

Community Newspapers

Rose Times/Cannonville News

The front doors were glass. The beefy EMT went inside and there some ditzy receptionist in a blue dress on the phone at the switchboard. Her hair was also raven and her skin very pale. Matt barely noticed. When the phone call ended she looked at him hungrily. There was a similar sign behind her. The room had ugly art, one cover framed, the first cover. There were two couches and a glass table with recent issues and there were more recent issues in front of her. "May I help you?"

He gave her the grin, which for some reason that always worked. "I'm here to see a writer named Justine," it took a moment. He had blanked. "Uh, Duchane."

"Political Columnist," she rattled off the location and directions from a large paper desk behind her faux marble counter. She tapped the visitor book in front of her. "You'll have to sign in." The receptionist grinned.

"Of course," he did and gave her the grin again. She ate it up.

"You're a friend right?" She was already going to let him in.

"Of course," *well I'd like to be.* The cute receptionist smiled at him and watched him go.

"Let's hope so," he whispered sarcastically and headed down a hall past a conference room and nice bathrooms. *Airhead.*

Benson was almost knocked over by the sheer number of people and desks. Everywhere. He couldn't keep track. *Guess I don't know much about newspapers.* Justine was found to be at her desk, reading a letter. She looked adorable with her nose crinkled and in her blue cream turtleneck. "A few good ideas I could pick apart," she said to herself.

She frowned at the big shadow, thinking it was someone else. "What Mac,"--then she looked up. Recognition filled her hazel eyes. "Is someone ill?"

"No Ma'am," the EMT tried cordiality and held out the flowers and gave her a pleasant smile. "I hope not, at least. Are you well?"

Duchane did not smile. "I'm fine," was the curt response. "What is this?"

"I'm Matt." Kelli peaked over her cube wall on the far end of the room. Lenor peaked out, impressed by the suitor.

"Happy for you." Justine looked at her typewriter.

"These are for you." His voice cracked and the political columnist eyed the flowers like they were snakes. "Was hoping that you may wish...want to have dinner with...or coffee with me er...with me, ever, sometime." What had sounded so suave in his head just came out as stammer and jumble of words. The big man was saying it all wrong. Kelli licked her lips and giggled, Lenor thought it was endearing.

"Let me get this straight," Justine leaned back in her gray office chair. "You came and interrupted my work to *flirt* with me?" The big handsome man shrugged. Lenor mirrored the gesture, thinking it was a very good thing. Kelli was admiring the EMT's fine ass.

"Well," no one accused Matt of being a poet and he was at a loss for words.

"You snuck back to the executive offices of a newspaper to *flirt* with me?" The political columnist looked almost as annoyed as she was.

That's when Benson saw the ring on her finger for the first time. She stood. There was something missing in front of him and Matt couldn't put his finger on it. "I just thought…" it was more of a mumble then a statement.

Duchane snatched the flowers and tossed them in the garbage. "Aren't you a medical professional?" There had been a column about medical privacy a year earlier.

"I'll walk you out," a sixty-year-old hand was put on Benson's shoulder and he turned to see Lenor. The older woman tried to give him a comforting look. But she hadn't spoken. They turned to see a large man in a silk suit, no tie, "come on," Mac told the younger man in a voice none of his employees had ever heard before.

"Theodore," his administrative assistant tried to protest but her employer put his arm around the EMT and led him away.

"It's still my paper," he looked at the more likable man, "walk with me." His voice did not sound asinine like it usually did.

When they were out of earshot the older woman looked at Justine. "I think you blew it." She trudged back to her desk with the first look of disdain the younger woman had ever given her. "An EMT," she made tisk tisk sound.

"What the hell does that mean?" Duchane asked Kelli, walking towards her.

Kelli Ann Jones, approaching, shrugged. "He was sweet, thoughtful, interested, has a good job and a better ass. I can't remember the last time a man brought me flowers."

Their voices were drowned out by the sound of typing in the next room as Maguire walked Benson out. "I think you made one mistake and only one mistake," the elder man explained.

"What is that?" The EMT was ashamed.

"Timing," that was a good enough answer. "You don't understand," an entirely different Maguire than the night before explained, "she's still in shock from last night. Your timing was not impeccable."

"Was it a headline today?" The editor shook his head.

"No. I also pulled some favors and buried the story with my competitors." Something had happened after Sully had hung up on Theodore Roosevelt Maguire. He had grown a conscious.

They entered the reception area and ignored the ditz behind the desk. Sorry, I shouldn't alliterate. "Why?" Matthew Jason Benson did not understand.

The editor shrugged. "Sometimes I have to do the right thing. She's been through enough." Maybe his humanity was salvageable.

"Um, sure," the EMT was more confused.

"Good luck," a hand was offered and the two big men shook hands,

Then the owner walked back through his newspaper surveying the many employees and decided he needed to get away for a while and rethink things. He past Justine's desk and was going to avoid bothering her and for once but she spoke to him first. Lenor had the Rose Hour open and Duchane was reading the Rose Times. The political theorist folded the page down and looked at him.

"Unknown woman attacked by criminal, unknown rescuer," she just studied Maguire's face. "You blew some serious sales."

"Do you really want your name in the paper for that?" barely looking back, he walked through his outer office. His columnist looked after him and watched him go, confused.

"No." It was loud as a whisper.

"Than for once I did the right thing," he looked at Yvette and Brianna. "You two go home, take two weeks off with pay," in matching low cut florals they watched him confused as he gently closed his inner office door behind himself.

Lenor followed him. She found him at the wet bar on one wall under various pictures of himself with the odd local celebrity. "Theodore?"

"Shut the door Miss Whatkins." He never called her that. Most of his coworkers didn't know her last name.

She asked the question that Justine was mouthing outside. "Why?"

"I don't know. I guess I realized last night I was more like the man in that alley than that handsome EMT." He swigged some forty-year-old scotch.

"Well damn it Mac, if you don't remind me of your father," she grinned. Senior Maguire had once been a junior reporter that Bad Vlad had fired for having a conscious.

"If you say so." He went to his uncle's chair. "You still have that friend, the head shrinker?"

"The one I met at the hospital when my husband died, yeah." She walked to the desk. "You are not like the man in the alley."

"I'm a prick." Lenor sat.

"Theo," no one but his parents called him that. "You are not…"

"What's the doc's name?" Mac finished his drink.

VIII

"Hey ya feelin' brother?" Bertram Bryan Booker asked. Hal was having his vitals checked by a cute a red haired nurse. Her scrubs were a pink, brought out her complexion. She eyed Book.

"I'm feeling good." The nurse's name tag read Jaime. Urban had started to fill the notebook. He flexed his hand, cramping. The pen was behind his ear, like he had done in high school.

"What's wrong with your hand?" Nurse Jaime asked. Booker licked his lips. She took the writer's hand and examined it.

"A couple of hours writing the old fashioned way," Horatio Albert Urban tapped the pad with his free hand.

"Haven't used those muscles in a long time?" Book came to the other side of his bed. Jaime reached in her pocket and produced a felt tip.

"Not like this," Hal chuckled.

"Speaking of writing," she reached for the heir to Billy Dee's hand and wrote her number on it. "Jaime, call me." She winked and went to leave the room.

Yeah, that's the way it was with the taller man.

"Discharge papers are on the table. Simple instructions for care, Dr. Burma's number is on there too." She disappeared and Book picked it up.

"Well shit," he mumbled confused.

"She made it official." Urban tapped the pad again.

An orderly knocked and entered with a push wheelchair. He was pastier than his white scrubs, almost albino. "I'm Rodney, do you need help with your shoes?" They were next to bed. Hal handed the pad and documents to his pal.

"You take care of these." He moved his legs, back in his jeans off the bed and stooped for his shoes. Rodney stooped to help him. "I'm good."

"Let me help you," He did. "Come on," he held a hand close as the writer shifted to the wheelchair.

"Oooh." He was still a bit dizzy. Book was laughing it up.

"Royal treatment." He handed the papers to his friend and patted his back.

"Forget anything?" The orderly asked.

"Nah," Hal explained and he was wheeled out of the room.

Rolling through the corridor Urban flipped through his notes and outline. He knew Booker was making eyes at women and they were swooning, the smaller man ignored it. The car was in the patient pick zone and Booker unlocked the passenger door. It was Chevy Camaro, red. Chick magnet. Hal shifted himself from the wheelchair to the seat. "Thanks Rod."

"Have a nice day," the orderly wheeled away. "Keep writing."

"What?" The writer asked in disbelief.

"Dr. Burma speaks too many," Rodney called back. The doors closed behind him automatically. Pretty high tech for 1988.

"Who is this Dr. Burma?" Book got in the driver seat and Hal shut his own door.

"She's a married doctor who told me to write," the writer explained. "And stop drinking."

"Married, aw nuts," the ebony Adonis drove away. "She got a sister?" Urban ignored him.

"Thanks for picking me up." He buckled up before they exited the parking lot.

"What are friends for, good buddy?" Book laughed. "Besides, Mac himself is paying for my gas. He also sent a check for the hospital."

"I don't get it." No one did. Captain Sarah Sullivan Hastings had really shamed Theodore Roosevelt Maguire.

Book just shrugged. "He said to make sure you're in tomorrow.

"I'm negative one sick day, I have to work anyway." A nod.

"Be ready at eight thirty I'm picking you up." Hal smiled.

"Can you help me with one other thing?" Booker glanced at his pal and made a turn.

"Course, what's up?" he asked.

"Take all the booze and beer from my apartment, dump it or take it home, but get every drop away from me..."

IX

"Clean desk clear mind,"Mr. Karlson had said.

"D-?" Hal had asked.

"You didn't have one."

"I don't understand."

"The paper is brilliant except the typos. You worked from a messy place."

"You can tell that from the paper?"

"Disordered desk, disordered mind."

"What does your workplace look like at home?"

"Kind of like this paper."

"I figured."

"I don't want to do this again."

"Clean your desk and you'll be doing A work." Karlson had grinned. *"Hal you are my favorite student. You have natural talent...use it."*

"I'm no William Shakespeare."

"Alas poor Bill, Horatio, no one is. But you could give Woody Allen a run for his money." The teacher had held out a pen. *"Write a Tony winner someday."*

"With this pen?"

"It's a symbol Mr. Opus."

Mr. Karlson had presented Hal with both his book award and a couple As.

That's why he cleaned his apartment before sitting down to write.

X

Theodore Roosevelt Maguire did not look at Justine as he walked by. "I told Lenor," who was following him, "to give you anything you need." He kept walking away.

That almost gave Duchane whiplash. "What was that?" She asked.

"How are you feeling young lady?" The matronly woman asked maternally, standing in front of the younger woman's cluttered desk.

"Did he just say what we think he did?" They watched the defeated man disappear.

"Yes he did." The political columnist crossed her arms.

"I'm fine. No injuries. I know what this," she scoffed. "Another ploy to get in my pants," Lenor shook her head.

"Not this time, anything you need after last night, just ask." Justine scratched her elbow.

"How do you know?" she asked.

"Do you know how long I've known the men in that family?" The younger woman just shrugged She was waiting for the punchline.

"Thirty, thirty five years?" Whatley threw back her head and laughed. "Forty?"

"Next month it will be forty-two years. Since the spring after I graduated high school." Whatley listed them; "Big Vlad, Bad Vlad, my friend Theodore Senior and finally Mac."

"Why do you put up with him?" Justine asked.

"Other than the contract I signed with his grandfather?" Lenor asked. A nod. "Bridget and I, Vlad's sister, went to high school together. She died in childbirth. He was an only child, raised by nannies."

"King Baby?" the columnist asked.

"Yes, but the last thing his mother told me was that he'd make us proud someday. She knew she had been carrying greatness. Then she was rolled into the operating room." The older woman wiped her eyes.

"Do you want me to pity him?" They looked at each other. "That it should condone all those years of bad behavior?"

"I didn't say that." Lenor held up a palsy hand. "He's made a baby step today; you have no idea how much what he did for you today cost him."

"I don't understand." Not many knew where the bodies were buried. Not many knew how to bury a story. Vlad had buried a story once in 1981, it was the right thing to do but for the wrong reasons, this was the second time she'd seen it.

"I've read your column; you know how the game is played in Washington. Backroom deals and favors... you build power with markers, who owes you." Duchane knew that, she had written that.

"It is...the way of power." Justine crinkled her nose. "People in power collect and dispense...oh." She realized. "How many did he call in?"

"All of them." Lenor gave her a moment for that to sink in. "Every last favor he and his uncle had built up. Mac probably did some begging... but no one knows." The truth is that if people saw her name in the paper the next question would be what does Justine write? Her pen name had been given many death threats… Hence she needed anonymity.

"If he had told me this, I never would have believed him," the political theorist explained.

"I know," Whatley agreed.

"What did he gain?" The younger woman asked.

"Something I don't think he's ever had. A moment of self-respect." The administrative assistant hesitated. "He treated you with respect. That's new for him. He's never done that with a woman before."

"What does he get from me?" Justine didn't plan to give him anything.

"Absolutely nothing. He made a purely redemptive act and he's better for it," the younger two secretaries filed past them silently and disappeared, never to be seen again at the paper again.

"It won't take." Justine was sure but Lenor laughed.

"Maybe and maybe not. But I think doing this for you made him better already." She turned to go back to work.

"How do I thank the sportswriter?" Duchane changed the subject.

"Who, Hal?" Lenor shrugged. "Fruit basket, maybe."

XI

Pamela Suzzette Tyler and Matthew Benson rolled a cardiac patient into The Emergency Department while another doctor was on duty. A pleasantly plump doctor named Shana accepted the patient. She had long brown hair and green scrubs. The septuagenarian was left in her care and the elderly woman's son stood off to the side of the ED waiting. Matt rolled the empty gurney back to the ambulance.

Pam went to the radio. "Seven oh one to base." *Damn Overtime.* They had returned to work at ten because of somebody's illness.

"Go Pam," Captain Jeremy Stabile responded.

"Package delivered. Do you need us at the moment?" She asked the boss her who still didn't trust her.

"No, why?" His voice crackled.

"We'll be here for a few if you need us," she told him.

"Go for it." Matt slammed the doors and studied the gray clouds in the ominous sky. Then he looked at his partner.

"What are you doing?" The younger woman shrugged. "What are we doing?"

"Food, grumpy pants." She laughed. Finally, Benson nodded. "Ice cream?"

"Why?" But they walked down the corridor, waiving to doctors, nurses and orderlies they knew. He just followed.

"You're down big guy. You need cheering up. Ice cream always works." She made herself laugh but he just kept walking. "Sheesh, tough audience."

"Alright." The doors opened and they crossed the hall to cafeteria. An impressive cafeteria in a state of the art medical center. They did not want pay for each other. They had strict rules about that.

Matt sat first at a round table. Next to a man in a suit, big cross worn over his tie, red bound book opened. He crossed himself, looked up and smiled. "Matthew."

"Deacon Jake." The book was closed and the men shook hands. Pam sat on her partner's other side. "This is my partner, Pamela."

"Ma'am." The head shrinker offered a hand.

"I'm not into the whole God thing," but she shook Jake's hand.

"That's okay." He leaned back and smiled paternally. "He believes in you anyway." No matter how many times Benson heard that, it always made him grin.

Tyler pushed her ice cream away. "Are you going to start the conversion speech?"

"Why?" The deacon sighed. "I respect the fact that you stand up for your opinions. In America you have the right to your opinion, just...know what it is."

"Deacon Jake is a psychologist on staff and has been for decades." Pond winced. Pam giggled. Ever since the old building he'd been shrinking heads. He was a shrink long before he was a deacon.

"Don't make me feel old Matthew." He put the book aside and pulled his apple pie towards himself.

"Nothing phases this man," Benson explained.

"What's your game?" Tyler tried to anyway. "Raping patients for money because you don't take insurance." The older man laughed.

"I have no game. I do take all insurances and I've spent my life helping patients that can't pay or could only pay scaled rates." He patted Matt's back. "That leads us to our friend here."

"Excuse me?" Benson asked, leaving ice cream on his chin. His partner picked up a napkin and wiped it off. "Thanks Pam." She just nodded.

"You don't think I don't recognize that look of perplexed anxiety." The head shrinker sighed. "Six years at URose, give me some credit."

"He got shot down and he hasn't been that interested in a babe in a long time," Pam told the sage bluntly.

"Oooh, angstful Romance," Jake rubbed his hands together. "I enjoy a good love story."

"You like chick stuff?" Tyler asked dejected.

"I'm an odd duck. My first date with my wife was a little movie called *Love Story* with Ryan O'Neal. Kind of set the tone. I'm a big fan of Richard Gere." He waited. "So tell me the truth Matthew. What's going on?"

"I saw something in this lady's eyes. She seems to be a wounded soul. I'd like to heal those wounds." His partner slapped her head and face palmed.

"All this from a few words and sentences. Gag me with a spoon." The big EMT pushed his ice cream away.

"Something just stuck out today. There's no picture of a fiancé on her desk, but she wears a ring. She never said 'I'm engaged,' when she threw me out of her office. Well, she was mad, her boss politely walked me out and said I just have bad timing."

"Timing is the secret of everything," the clergyman agreed.

"That in the Bible, Rev?" Tyler asked.

He laughed. "No ma'am. That's Lyndon Baines Johnson." She had no comeback for that. "You want a story an agnostic told me Pam?" He asked.

"Um, sure?" she was dejected.

"In nineteen forty-two a certain young man, just eighteen was drafted into the US army to be sent to The Pacific. At his last stop he had a layover in San Francisco and he went out with friends at a presidio bar--eighteen for drinks. You know, like in the old movies?" They nodded. "At a bar filled with servicemen and dames," that elicited chuckles, "he saw a lady, in candy striper garb, reading a letter over and over again. When she finally put it away and her drink was low the soldier walked over and offered to buy her a drink."

"And they lived happily ever after?" The younger EMT asked.

"She shot him down," the speaker went on. "He was humiliated. So he had another beer and stopped at the bathroom before exiting the back door to head back to barracks. He found the same lady crying over the letter. He apologized and she apologized. She told him she hated crying in public. Her beau had just been killed in a part of the World she could not pronounce."

"Oh my God," Matt commented.

"He was infantry, shot in the night. Well, shit happens in war," they ignored the curse, "You know, what they say... anyway she explained it was bad timing. He gave her his handkerchief and walked away after an enriching conversation never even getting her name but her face was etched in his memory for three years at war."

"That's a terrible story," Tyler complained.

"Yes, it would have been but sometimes The Universe or God or Fate or Buddha or Dumb luck or The Force or insert whatever the heck want to insert here has other ideas," they waited. "After the war, the hero was on a layover in Portland Oregon and in the airport he recognized a face across the terminal."

"Same girl?" Pam was panting with pregnant expectation. Sorry, alliteration again.

"They're son owns Pennyless Video."

"Timing?" The audience asked together.

"Timing."

THURSDAY

Seemingly without explanation Justine Anabeth Duchane was in the sports department. She approached the sportswriter's desk. He had only missed the one day, apparently. Horatio Albert Urban's throat tightened. "Hal?" She asked him.

It's not that he didn't find her attractive, she was just plain beautiful. It's that she terrified him. He felt she was aloof. He did, however, honestly believe she had the right to be. However, as strange as it looked she had a small smile on her face. "Mmmhmm."

"How's the head?" A bit tentatively she put her hand on the cubicle side wall. Was she nervous? He didn't know she ever felt that way.

The writer didn't reach for the stitches. "It beats a hangover."

Book kept his eyes on his typewriter but listened in. He was typing local sports, 'Thorns over McMahon…' he had a knack for making high school sports exciting.

"I'm glad you're in today…and okay," the political theorist shifted her weight.

"No more sick time," the nervous man studied her eyebrows.

"Hal," Justine bit her lips. She wore beige capris, a tan blouse. He had a tucked in blue dress shirt and clean jeans on. "*You* did save *me.*" As hard as it was to believe.

The writer looked away. He didn't have the balls to look her in the eye. What had John Wayne said about courage? She quoted The Duke a lot. "Well, don't mention it."

"I *have* to mention it, it's important." He shifted in his chair and looked past her face. "I'm in your debt Hal."

"No, no. Not at all." His head twinged. Writer, not talker.

"Um, is the hospital paid?" Booker wheeled his chair around. Strangely, she respected the womanizer, she didn't get that either.

"It was taken care of," the velvet voice answered for his friend.

"Really, Justine, I'm happy if you leave it in the past," Urban argued. "I appreciate you coming down here, but you're welcome."

Duchane furrowed her brow. She didn't know what to say. Was he right? Was that all that needed to be said? "Why do you men pretend?"

"Why do you hate people?" The small pasty man answered without thinking.

"It's not that I hate people, it's that I...I don't socialize." *Well I'm done with dating and I hate bullshit and and...* Who was she trying to convince?

"Sorry, Justine. That came out of wrong. Your 'socializing' is none of my business." Urban face palmed, embarrassed. Book turned around again.

Duchane laughed. "It's rare to find a man who neither tries to hit on me nor doesn't want to talk about my sex life."

"As I said," he grinned sheepishly.

"Hal," she leaned forward and whispered in his ear. "I'm not a lesbian." Justine straightened. They had a bit of an audience now.

"Okay." What else was he going to say?

"I don't date Hal. I'm not hitting on you or trying to chat you up." Finally, the political theorist got to her point. "However I think I should do something to make us square." Book turned again, curious.

"Please, I don't want you to feel obligated to me in any way," the writer looked at his typewriter nervously. "I can't ask you for anything, I don't have the right."

"You're not, I'm offering." She was at that. "I'm telling you that I am going to do something to make us square." Suddenly the soft fluorescent lighting made Hal sweat. Justine didn't like the uneasy feeling all this gave her. She was opening up too much. Still she had the uncontrollable urge to square the debt. It's like she was honor bound and it was a debt of honor. *How odd?*

"We're good, Miss Duchane," Mr. Urban told her.

"Why don't you just ask her Hal?" Bertram B. Booker barked.

"Tell me what?" Justine asked both of them. There was a larger audience now.

"He can't make a drive this weekend, no vehicle, and he's crestfallen," the best friend made clear. A road trip isn't quite what she meant.

"Car in the shop?" She asked. *Oh what the hell? I could take him in a fight.*

"And unreliable," the writer explained with a forced grin. "But you shouldn't--I mean I don't want--that is I don't expect…" a great *verbal* communicator he was not. At least when he was scared or nervous or drunk.

"So, where do you want to go?" The tall woman asked, shifting her weight.

"Massachusetts, just west of Riverside Park. It's an old school movie theater that is showing a Joseph Cotten film festival this weekend." That actually perked Hal up. "I like to see those stately old movies in the stately old theaters they were filmed for."

At first the political theorist just crinkled her nose. Then she remembered the name. *"Citizen Kane?"* She thought out loud.

"Um, yeah, but more like *Portrait of Jenny* and several others. Those writers were playwrights." Book turned back to his column.

"Why aren't you taking him Bertram?" he whirled.

"Shhh...lady keep that name on the down low." She actually grinned at that. "Girl, there is a suite at the Waldorf, reservations at Top of the Sixes and Yankee tickets waiting for a lady,"--but Justine was already cutting him off.

"I get it Booker," Duchane sighed and Book went back to his column, again.

"Well, it's just some old movies in Massachusetts," Hal started typing. "It's not important." It was the last thing, he thought, in his shitty life, that he really liked.

"Is there a hotel or reasonable B and B nearby?" for some reason Justine was still asking questions. The writer typoed again. *Shit.*

Urban looked up confused. "There are two or three good hotels close--and oh yeah, one beautiful B and B." He never had stayed there, two expensive.

"Doesn't the B and B have private rooms?" Then and only then did Horatio Albert Urban allow himself to have any hope.

"Of course the Motel 6 would be cheaper," *not to mention less romantic,* he concluded.

"Do you have the festival tickets yet?" He opened his desk drawer. "First show is eight PM

Friday night." The tickets were inside a program, sticking out of an envelope.

"Two nights in Massachusetts?" Justine Anabeth Duchane asked.

"Last show is Sunday in the afternoon. *Kane, Portrait of Jenny, Third Man, Shadow of a Doubt. September Affair, Duel in the Sun, Under Capricorn* and *Peking Express.*" That was quite a program.

"Not *Magnificent Ambersons?*" She asked.

He shrugged. "It's not an Orson Welles festival, that was last year."

"Good. I hate that movie." He shrugged. "What?"

"Welles may have been a middling actor and a tyrannical director, but he could sure write and he certainly influenced me." Absently a hand wandered to a notebook he'd been working in.

"Good. I'll drive and pay for two rooms at the B and B, you pay for gas and food. Then we're even. Deal?" She held out her hand.

"Justine?" Hal looked confused at her hand.

"*Deal.*" It was not a question. It was a final decision.

"Deal." They shook on it.

"Good choice. *Portrait of Jenny* is one of my favorite old movies." That made the writer actually grin. She hadn't known Cotten's name.

"Um...erm.." he was at a loss for words though. *Thank you seems inadequate.*

"It's not a date, it's a ride," the political theorist decreed.

"I swear," the writer agreed.

"Good." She turned to go.

"But Justine?" He started to ask.

"What?" She paused and looked over her shoulder. She looked very feminine like that.

"Are you sure?" She nodded.

"You were the other night."

FRIDAY

Deacon Jake sat in Dr. Liz Burma's office. "Any luck finding Mister Flaherty a kidney?" she asked. He raised an eyebrow.

"*I'm* not the one trying." He a shook his head. "It's a hard match."

The physician rubbed the space on her nose between her eyes. "Too bad. That young man is a nice guy with so much ahead of him." She leaned back and Pond stood.

"I'm seeing a new patient today." She waited. "I don't want to be biased and you went to high school with him." Liz stood.

"Now you have to tell me, this is *my* hospital." a wave of his hand.

"Everyone can change Lizzy," he opened the door and went to meet Mac Maguire.

XII

Justine Anabeth Duchane pulled her Volvo onto Interstate 95 North. Horatio Albert Urban sat in the passenger seat watching the southern New England trees. She had two Poland Spring single serve bottles in the cup holder and the car was immaculate. In the glove compartment her cassettes were alphabetized and she had WEBE 108 FM on the radio, but low. Even the trunk was spotless, he had seen when he'd put his duffel bag with her suitcase. It was 5:05 PM Friday night.

"Um, nice car," was all the writer could think to say.

"Thanks," she wore loose jeans, black sneakers and black turtle necked sweater. She didn't look at him.

Hal was in jeans and an old Mets shirt, something he'd picked up in a work promotion--that was most of his wardrobe. His sneakers were also scuffed. They had once been white. "Lease or finance?" He was trying too hard now. Small talk had always been hard for him. That made the driver snort. "Or trust fund?"

That last one actually made Justine laugh and it lightened the mood. "Lease."

It was in good shape. "Impressive." Truthfully, he knew nothing about buying and leasing new cars. There was silence in the car for a moment. "Did you grow up in Cannonville?" He had heard somewhere that her townhome was in town. He wasn't far away in Rose.

Small talk? Justine asked herself. *I guess we're going to do this.* "Cannonville High School class of seventy-six," she admitted.

"Saint M's class of seventy-seven." She had to give him credit, he was trying, unfortunately he had just made her feel old.

Now it was her turn. She bit her lip. "Book told Kelli you were a theater major?"

He had stayed close to his parents. They were in Cannonville actual, he barely saw them though. "Basically, what about you?" They had a long drive to fill.

"Poli-Sci," she gave him the Reader's Digest version. She looked out her window at the bastion of liberalism Connecticut was becoming and sighed. Despite her conservative views she had achieved first honors at a public university. It would always be an uphill climb for her.

Of course now she wrote for liberal newspaper and was sitting in her car with a borderline alcoholic who probably never had voted in his life. "Was this the job you planned on?" *Damn it, now he gets insightful.* Planned on? They both knew that was just another phrase for pipe dream.

"Planned on? What, writing for this rag?" Justine crinkled her nose again.

"Me neither." Hal looked at the window again and was wondering if he'd have enough words for the play he was writing. He could have sworn the words were there a decade ago.

"What did you hope for?" That question made the writer cringe.

"Do you care?" The political theorist looked out the window silent for a moment.

"It's a long drive Hal, let's fill it up." That was a really good point. It also didn't answer his question and opened up a whole other can of worms. "Are you going to write?"

"You think I should?" Good question.

"Yes," was a quick reply and only then did she realize she meant it.

"You're the second woman to tell me that this week," Hal admitted.

"Who was the other?" Justine changed lanes. He told her. "And?" Don't get me wrong, neither of them were one hundred percent invested in the conversation.

"Well, I've filled her pad. When I go back to get the stitches out she wants to see the full play." He leaned back in his chair watching the cars pass on the left and be passed on the right. That was life wasn't it? Oh that was good, he had to remember that.

"You must have written before?" He shrugged. "In college?"

"And was published once, sort of, but it's been a long time." He still felt stale when he wrote. Maybe it was rust, maybe not. "I started a play about the life of a failed father, an obsessed Yankee fan."

"You never wear a Yankee hat," Justine observed. *What a stupid thing to say! Damn where is my head?*

"No, but I have Yankee pajamas," for the first time they shared an honest laugh. "The Yanks are the only team I really care about--but this sports thing--I'm an artist. I never played ball...I wouldn't watch it regularly if I wasn't paid to. I prefer to write fiction."

"Who said you had to give up your dream?" She almost scoffed at herself, Justine realized she was sounding an awful lot like her mom.

"Who said you did?" He fired back. *Ooops.* Hal had called her bluff.

There was a long tangible silence. The pasty man looked at at the beautiful woman and she actually seemed interested in the conversation now. "What kind of stories?" Quick save.

"Not the kind that make big Hollywood money per say. I'd rather write Broadway or local theater. A place where a writer can thrive." It had been a long time since the writer had thought of these things; but now he spoke of them.

"Why not Hollywood?" Urban laughed out loud. "What's so funny?"

"Name five American playwrights." That made Duchane stop and think.

"Um...Neil Simon." He chuckled.

"Cop out, go on." She changed back to the right lane to exit onto a different interstate.

It took a moment, "Arthur Miller?"

The writer smiled. "Good catch. but why do you know his name?" A blank look appeared on her face. "Can you name one of his plays or one of his wives?"

"Uh," *sorta,* "Marilyn." The political columnist felt foolish.

"Exactly. Another?" She sneered.

"Woody Al,"--she stopped. "Ugh!" She crinkled her nose and even let out a small giggle.

"All three of them are movie men, made money in Hollywood. Only Woody kept control of his work, but their all sell outs." She could only nod blankly.

"What's wrong with that?" Fair question. "It's a living."

"I'll name four movies, if you can name the screenwriters I'll concede your point, Okay?" She looked at him briefly.

"Deal." He laughed.

"*Empire Strikes Back, Jaws, Out of Africa* and an easy one *Love Story.*" Justine smiled. She believed he had tipped his hand.

"George Lucas, Steven Spielberg, Robert Redford and... damn, I don't know." Hal laughed out loud.

"You got them all wrong." Her eyes went open wide. "*Empire* was adapted from an original outline by the executive producer, George Lucas, he does not have screenwriter credit. Spielberg has only written one movie, *Close Encounters,* then he stopped writing. Redford is an actor and sometimes director, he never ever writes. He also did not direct *Out of Africa. Love Story* was adapted by Erich Segal, from his novel-- geared to the director's desires."

"I didn't know that," she got back in the center lane.

"Did you care?" They laughed.

"No." He hadn't thought so. "So what's wrong with movie money?" The political theorist eyed the writer skeptically. "You don't like money?"

"There's nothing wrong with money. Arthur Miller money would be fine. Being married to Kim Basinger would be cool too." They laughed. "I don't need Neil Simon money."

"So what's wrong with movie writers?" Duchane waited, but Urban didn't answer right away. "And why don't I know them?"

"That's exactly the problem with movie writers." He sighed. "I love movies, just don't want to write them." She waited. "Writers don't write them anyway."

"What do you mean?" Justine had finally met someone more opinionated than she was. Well, maybe as opinionated.

"Oh sure they present dialogue, and some semblance of a script---sometimes. Then studio executive dictate what gets shown. The director controls what gets filmed, actors complain and ad lib. Often everything is decided on, pre-production is done and cameras are rolling before the final 'script,' is completed." He made quotation gestures.

"Always?" That disappointed the driver.

"Depends," the passenger began. "But *Star Wars, Indiana Jones, Lethal Weapon and Silverado* are all kinds of fun. Directors like Lucas, Spielberg, Donner and Kasdan are richer than God. In Hollywood they have that kind of power, of course the almighty executive controls movies. There are very few true filmmakers and I know of no writer that got exactly what he intended on the screen since the talkie era began."

"Wow," there's a column and a half.

"Film is a director's medium. TV is a producer's medium. Japanese theater is an actor's medium. Our theater, like England's, is a writer's medium. I'm a writer, not a puppet." He had said and it he had meant it. Horatio Albert Urban was a writer again. He had also earned Justine Anabeth Duchane's respect.

"Why not a novel?" That was a very fair question.

"I can't write prose for shit." She laughed out loud.

"So how long has it been since you finished a play?" Hal got very quiet.

"Eight years." He looked out the window. "But I have a full working outline of *Nine Innings of Life*. This doctor has pushed me that far."

"That's an interesting title. How is it laid out?" She liked a good story.

"Jewish man. His ninety-year journey to become a good man. Ninety years, nine innings I based him on my Uncle Hal and my grandfather Lazar." He liked his grandfather, couldn't stand his uncle.

"Odd title. Unique format. Does have the play take place on the field or at a game?" He chuckled. Astute.

"You guessed it perfectly." Giggling, a unique and pleasant sound, she rapped the wheel. "Well done." They laughed.

She took a sip of water. "Uh-huh." She raised an eyebrow. "You have an Uncle Hal?" "Oh, you hate him." Justine frowned.

"Opus, that liberal First Selectman, we all know is a crook, but can't prove it." Urban got very very ashamed for a moment. Opus was the first selectman, small town mayor, of Cannonville.

"I don't like him either." Duchane sighed. "I can read people. He's a villain. You aren't." She looked at him for a second. "I've also read your column. While I don't vote, you make many good points." That brought the conversation to a whole new level. "You're the hero."

"Hmm. Give me an example, writer. How am I hero?" He hesitated. "Go on."

"I understand your thought process. I read your article about building the new Joselof elementary for a few millions of taxpayer money when we could have rented Saint Joseph's school for a dollar a year and maybe ten grand of remodeling. The town council voted eight to two to build a new building. That showed me that you know how to manage money and you stand against those who would empty our wallets." There was a pause. "You have something politicians don't."

"What? A conscious?" Justine asked laughing. This was the most talking Hal had done in years. "Just out of curiosity, what did you mean by thought process?"

"Well, you began with a joke, how everyone loves Cannonville schools on September first but hates them on April fifteenth. Then you bring in an off the wall factual reference which reminds your audience that you know exactly what you're talking about." *He has really read my stuff. Maybe he should be writing a play about me.* But the writer paused.

"Go on."

"You also write as one of your readers, not as an ivory tower liberal intellectual. You use simple English." *Wow!* He may or may or not be hitting on her, but no one had given Justine a compliment like that in.

she couldn't remember when. "You remind me of Truman, plain, simple and straightforward."

"He was a democrat," Justine corrected him.

"Okay." Hal shrugged. "So what did you want to be?"

The driver shook her head. "Oh no," come the half-hearted protest.

"Oh come on, I fessed up," the writer argued. Urban tried to give the political theorist the smolder and it just made her laugh.

They both realized how comfortable they had become during that drive so Duchane opened up. She never opened up. "Alright. Okay," she fidgeted in her seat and that made him laugh. "When I was a little girl I dream of something very different than most little girls--or little boys." This had to be good.

"I take it that you didn't want to be a fairy princess?" She laughed. That was a good joke. "GI Joe?" She laughed again.

"GI Joe? Really?" He laughed. "Alright, fine." She decided to say it. "I've always dreamed of being governor of Connecticut."

Hal thought long and hard. "I know this will sound weird from a guy that forgot to register to vote but I think you should do it. You would make one hell of a governor."

"Um, thanks, why?" That made her shy again.

"Everyone thinks I'm just the idiot who screws up the sports column Justine. I do read our paper. I know Connecticut is broken." Now he was embarrassed. "But the mind who writes your column is exactly the hero in the play I'd write about fixing this crazy state of ours."

"Aren't you apolitical?" He chuckled.

"Oh well, no one's perfect." Hal shrugged. "Lazy, not stupid." That about summed him up. "You turned out to be a lot more articulate and personable in real life than I expected." He slapped his mouth. "Sorry."

"No it's okay. I know I hide behind walls. I don't want to be a total bitch… it's just." That when the writer saw it. "I've been hurt." Justine stopped talking.

"Okay. You don't have to tell me about it." He looked ahead. In all the time they'd been working together Hal had never said anything flirtatious and was respectful and kind and honest as he'd been, lapping the praise, Justine didn't hate the vibe from him in the car.

"Kurt was my fiancé. He screwed up." She didn't go into detail. "Four years ago."

"So you wear the ring to scare men off?" He realized that that would make a great plot device, so the writer made a mental note.

"Hell no. I pawned that ring for a stereo." They laughed. "As you said, I'm a smart girl. This is a glass replacement to scare men off."

"I'm sorry."

"Why? You didn't hurt me." That was true and then she spoke the truth she'd been fighting for years. "All men didn't hurt me. One did." *So why have I been blaming all men?*

"Um...thank you." He was nervous again. "I didn't expect you to share." She shrugged.

"Don't use my name in a play." They laughed. "Get *Nine Innings* staged." His brain started turning, on overdrive. He had a beautiful idea. An awesome, beautiful idea.

There was a long silence. "How does one become governor?" Justine raised an eyebrow.

"How does one get become a staged playwright?" Hal shrugged now.

"He submits to theaters and then works his way up. I asked first." Yes, he had.

"Yes you did." The political theorist bit her lip. "You submit your name for town council. One thousand signatures and you are on the ballot. You get elected. You don't forget to get your name in the paper. Then state rep, state senate and then governor."

Hmmm. The writer's brain worked. "When is the next seat open on the Cannonville Town Council?" The driver laughed.

"Whoa boy, this is not one of your plays." No it wasn't. He *could* help her.

"Well, D is an early letter, is the ballot alphabetically like in the movies?" The passenger asked. He had another thought.

"Yes, but,"--maybe he was writing an ending for her. "Huh?"

"You wrote a column about the uniformed American voter who votes for the first name or names on the ballot." She had written that. To help her he was using her own words against her. He was good when he was sober.

"Look Hal, I'm flattered that you read my columns, but...I." He shook his head.

"Justine. We're too old for could bes and maybes and might have beens." She had heard something like that before. "You have a dream and I have a dream, I'll help you if you help me." She scoffed. But it wasn't a pick up line. She glanced at him.

"How?"

"You help me get staged I'll help you get elected to town council." That was a deal of the millennium. He also couldn't be serious.

"What? Hal no." She pulled off into a service station for drive thru dinner.

"Yes. I'll keep writing if you campaign." Stopped in line, she looked at him. "I'll be your campaign manager you proofread my plays." Killing two birds with one stone.

"I run, you write. No matter the outcome?" The writer nodded.

XIII

Deacon Jake Pond's office was a borrowed office at Saint M's Hospital. Three chairs that didn't wheel, an almost empty desk and a window behind the client that faced a brick wall. He had been borrowing it exclusively since before his PhD, about twenty-five years. There was a picture of him and his wife with their two kids, Harry and Leia and that was it. Pond was obsessed with all things George Lucas. He wore a light brown suit and matching tie. Theodore Roosevelt Maguire Jr. faced him.

"I have to admit the cross makes me...uncomfortable." Mac was surprised that that made the psychologist laugh.

He reached for pectoral ornament. "I could take it off."

"Really?" The head shrinker pulled the gold chain out from under his dress collar and removed the jewelry. Then he put it in the side pocket of his suitcoat.

"Better?" He was over fifty and his children were under ten. He and his wife had been...blessed late with kids.

"Wow, I don't get you clergy folks." The editor was wide eyed.

"I'm your secular mental health professional right now." He sighed. "This is our second meeting and you still haven't told me why."

"I'm unhappy." The bigger arms were crossed. I say it like that because it's debatable who the bigger man really was. Mac dwarfed Jake physically, but--you fill in that blank.

"Why?" *Damn shrinks.* But the sage was wise. He'd cracked tougher nuts in this office. "Okay, I see that perturbs you. Humor me and guess."

"I'm...I'm oversexed." No reaction. "Aren't you shocked?"

"I have Aids patients Mac, you're an amateur. If you're trying to shock me you're going to have to try much harder." In the psych ward with methadone, suicidal delusionists and people dying of all kinds of horrible diseases in the hospital Dr. Jacob Pond had heard it all twice.

"Oh really?" The younger man tried to impersonate Bad Vlad. He failed.

"Do you want to shock me? Do you need to shock anyone?" Jake asked. He smoothed his thinning hair. Nervously Maguire looked out the window.

"The other night I was watching porn when my phone rang... I learned about the incident of River Street." Pond waited. "I knew the cop. I went to high school with her. Damn St. M's high school." It was the best private school in the area and it was across the street. "The way she told me...it shamed me. I smashed my TV."

"Incident on River Street?" The deacon asked.

"One of my employees was almost assaulted and another got stitches rescuing her. Damn scrawny writer." He almost chuckled.

Scrawny writer, Stitches. The pieces came together. "Why did you smash the TV? You weren't committing any crimes."

Mac scratched his chin. "Aren't you supposed to question my morals and offer me penance or something?" The atheist was confused.

"The is psychology, not Confession," Jake laughed. "You don't need a lecture either. I still want to know why you smashed the TV."

"The girl in alley...I...I've been sexually harassing her since day I met here. Women and me...I talk a big game. I pay for it...I take and take and take. I'm selfish..." The editor's voice kept cracking.

"Hmmm," The sage leaned on his chin. "Have you ever given something to anyone just for the sake of giving it?"

Mac leaned back offended. "What? Your church need money or something?" Unmoved Pond reached for his wallet.

"I don't mean money--and we're doing very well thank you very much. I mean like a kind word, a smile, a gift." He pulled a card from the pocket. It read 'blood donor,' and something like twelve gallons. "Blood, for example. Doesn't cost you anything but time and every pint saves three lives." Maguire face palmed.

"I tell you I'm unhappy and you tell me to give up a part of my body." Part of the body? Really? He said pint of blood. But, unoffended, Jake replaced his wallet.

"No. But I know why you're unhappy. I know how it can be fixed, but it won't be easy and you will have to do a lot of work," *finally the reverend gets to the point!*

"So why am I unhappy?" Mac waited for everything and all things he wanted to be given to him--as he had for forty years, not seeing the problem in front of his face.

"You are selfish prick who makes himself unhappy." The words were even and lucid and they just about made Theodore Roosevelt Maguire fall out of his chair. *Can he call me that?*

"What the hell?" Deacon Pond shrugged.

"I've sat in this office for more than two decades and do you know what my patients have taught me?" The sage asked.

"How to talk down to us?" But he knew he was wrong the moment he said it. There was a long pregnant pause in the conversation "What?"

"Sel*fish* people are miserable. Sel*fless* people are filled with joy." He smiled. "I don't mean money. I don't even mean kidneys...I just mean simple charity, a kind look, a pat on the back, respectful words edification when someone needs it."

"Your Cath'lic Bible teach you that Reverend?" Pond laughed. He did not officially go by Reverend Mr. Jacob Joseph Pond. He went by Dr. Pond at work, or Jake.

"No. My *patients* taught me that and if you open your eyes you'll see someone very close to you lives that *with* you." The sage interlocked his fingers, leaned back and waited.

"Who?" Mac scoffed. "God?"

"I have not brought religion into this conversation once." Maguire thought about that for a long long time. The head shrinker waited, they had time left.

"Holy shit!" The older man waited. "*You* haven't."

"Think hard Theodore. What women have you been closest to... ever. Forty years what woman has been the one constant." Pond didn't move.

Mac rolled his eyes. "Lenor?" No one spoke. "She can be real hard on me."

"This is my family." Jake leaned forward and picked up the picture. Leia and my little knight, Harry." He pointed the boy, a tall fair haired boy of nine. "He's a real daredevil. Sometimes I think those stunts will kill him. Sometimes I have to yell, sometimes he gets punished and I know he thinks I'm being hard on *him*."

They let that sink in and the seconds ticked by. The only clocks in the room were the shrink's Timex and the editor's Rolex. "But you're giving him what's good for him..."

"Lenor knows all about giving and she's a happy woman." Mac scratched his head.

"Wait a minute. You met her here. She's your friend, isn't she Jewish?" The deacon smiled. "She is Jewish."

XIV

Justine spoke, "it's a long time since a man said and did things that made me feel better without wanting something physical in return." That stopped him.

"Um you're welcome," Hal started, "I don't understand."

"Well," Justine sighed, "Men never do." They both nodded. "You don't creep me out Hal, don't worry." That made him feel better. "Hell you, actually make me feel comfortable. You don't do most of the dude things that get under my skin."

"Well," the writer laughed, "I leave that to Book." The car almost shook with shared laughter. Yeah, the handsome friend had testosterone poisoning.

"Do you have a girlfriend Hal?" *Oh crap.* He couldn't remember the last time he'd had a date. There was a long pause as Urban searched for an answer. "Has it been that long?" Duchane asked knowingly. Why write? She read him like a book.

"Um…" the breath was steady. "It was when I saw *Platoon*. That rental was my last date with a girlfriend.so what, early last year. Hell, Ellis at Pennyless Video could look it up in the computer." Well, I could.

"Oh-hoh! Name drop. You rent from Doyle too?" Richard Blaine Doyle was a former marine who owned Pennyless Video, Ellis Bennett worked for him.

"Don't we all?" He looked out the window. "It's been that long? God damn I've been in the bottle too long." Hal sighed.

"What about Ellis?" She asked.

"Um.no. We have a mutual respect at a distance policy, ever since high school. Plus I think she has a boyfriend." The scenery rolled by. "Damn bottle."

"My uncle Charlie was a binge drinker Hal, not an alcoholic. I think you're like him. He'd go a decade without a drink all my himself. After my aunt died from Friday night to Monday morning he'd get drunk and stay drunk at the drop of a hat. I never saw him inebriated though nor did his employees. My dad told me all this. Charlie could take it or leave it. But he was afraid to be sober all weekend…" the politician wiped an eye. "Wow, I've never shared this with anyone."

"If it's,"--she cut him off.

"He wasn't an alcoholic. They don't have a choice. He did. You have a choice. You chose to hide. We've worked together a long time Hal; I've seen you around. An alcoholic would beg, steal, trade, prostitute themselves or borrow for the next drink. That's not you."

The writer sighed. "I guess not. Hmm. Something right about me."

"Good." She patted his shoulder. Not the first time she'd touched him, but the first he'd remember. He didn't react.

"What happened to Charlie?" The story seemed to not have an ending yet.

"He met Aunt Olga. He's returned to the way he was before his first wife, the one I never knew died. He's never been drunk again. But he toasts at parties and weddings...always a choice for him. He's making better choices now. He met her because he and dad moved their business to Chicago, Supply Chain Ltd."

"So I need someone?" Hal was not happy.

"Or something to believe in," Justine suggested. "Believe in your writing."

"Hmmm." As they entered Massachusetts they realized they were talking like old friends.

"So why Joseph Cotten?" She asked.

"He chose good writers." That made her laugh. What else did she expect?

"Do you watch TV?"

"Who doesn't?" She giggled.

"I am big fan of The Cosby Show and I'm obsessed with M*A*S*H." He smiled.

"Best writing TV ever had. Television will never have another Alan Alda. He could write, direct, be funny, be serious. I have so much respect for his talent," Hal was fawning.

"He's a liberal," Justine argued.

"Do you love his work?" The writer asked.

"Yes." The politician grinned. "*Touché* I'm a fan of his work. What about Star Trek?"

"Kirk or Picard?" It was 1988 most people wouldn't even acknowledge the first spinoff.

Duchane wasn't everyone

XV

The movie theater had been built in 1898 for music and stage. It started showing movies in 1912, they had records of showing *Birth of Nation* and while the film offends most people, it is the oldest American film still intact. By the time *Wings* had won best picture; National Theater was only showing movies. In the fifties drive-ins stole business and in 1982 it had gone chapter 11. Two unmarried women in their thirties borrowed money from their daddies in 1983 and done their best to restore it. They had turned it into a second run and classics theater that had two annual festivals. It turned a profit.

It was a stately wooden building with an old school marquee on each side of the widow's walk. The windows were small and the paint was chipping but the bathrooms were clean. The urinals were so old they went from chest to floor. There was a new popcorn maker and they sold candy. It was staffed only by part time employees. The taller owner, Paula, blonde and slim wore an old time red usher's suit and introduced every film. She was a wealth of knowledge.

The Wickert Bed and Breakfast was a cute old Victorian three story that always promised breakfast to those who were up early enough. There was one set of adjoining rooms on the second floor and Justine had booked them. They checked in and saw the first movie. Then Duchane said "goodnight," and bolted her door. Hal wrote late, took his pants off and slept in his underwear.

SATURDAY

Of course the writer overslept. That evil snooze button. The knock on the door awoke him. "Fifteen minutes Hal!"

He heard the shower go on so Horatio Albert Urban sat on the bed for a minute and rubbed his eyes. "Lazar and Ira. Father and sons. Baseball." He liked what he had written so far. Then he pulled on a fresh shirt and blue sweater. He wore Friday's jeans.

He was tying his shoes when she knocked again. "Ready."

"Come in." She opened the door. Ponytail. No makeup; no surprise. Her pants were khaki and her sweater cream. Same flats as the day before. She eyed the papers and notebooks everywhere.

"You've been busy." She eyed one page. "Good." Then she looked at him. "Hungry?"

"I could eat." He stood, grinning.

"Let's do that." It's a good idea." Don't like the mess, glad you've been busy." Mr. Karlson would be disappointed. They left through his door.

"Sleep well?" But he had heard her TV most of the time he'd been writing.

"Well enough." They went downstairs to oak dining room with breakfast bar and big sparsely filled table. There was a grandfather clock.

She poured black coffee. "You don't have to answer but do you have insomnia Justine?"

Duchane was pouring cereal. She looked over the bowl at Urban. "Yeah, why?" But it was a grin and not a frown. "Why? Was my TV too loud?"

"No, not at all. I was writing anyway," he assured her. She sat on one side of the table between a girl in pigtails and red sweater as well as teenaged boy with a Walkman in wearing a Springsteen sweatshirt.

He sat between an old man in gray cardigan and bowtie reading the paper and a forty something year old woman in simple red and white dress that was probably the pigtailed girl's mom. "You too Hal?" He shrugged. "Sober and all?"

"Mmmhmm." He had bread and butter. The breakfast of champions.

"I'm sorry." The Writer shook his head.

"For what? Staying up all night watching TV? Should I apologize for staying up all night writing?" Duchane laughed at that and took a bite of corn flakes.

"That's true. No one was harmed." He had coffee as well, light and sweet.

"So how are *we* going to go about this town council thing?" He had stressed *we*. He was in for more than a suggestion. That amazed her.

"We?" The politician crinkled her nose.

"I give you my services, two hundred percent," Hal assured her. "*I* don't write if *you* don't run." She had made that deal hadn't she?

Justine smirked. "Do you even have a Cannonville address?"

"No. But I have a phone." He chuckled.

"Well, that's a start. But you can't vote for me. You're going to work for someone you can't even vote for?" He shrugged. "You don't vote anyway, do you?"

"Nope." He laughed. "You said you need signatures."

"Yes." The writer nodded.

"Well, I can canvas Walbaum's and I can get Book to do the same thing, women love him. We'll fill your petition in one day." The politician chuckled.

"I'd like to see that." All the pasty man could do was shrug. "I'd like to see your play too." That made the writer pause a bit.

"That's the deal." By the way, women fake smiles too. She gave him one.

"I appreciate that," but it was a lie. She was already having second thoughts. *I can't run for office. This is a pipe dream.*

"I hit a wall last night. All those papers and then a wall." Urban had reread twice and didn't know what to write next.

"You need a date." *What is she playing matchmaker?*

"What? Are you going to be my wingman Justine?" They laughed.

"Why not?" She looked out the window at an oak tree. Then she took her ring off. "When we get back I'm going to ask a man out." She put in her pocket.

"Whom?" Hal was curious. The politician blushed, she actually blushed.

"Um." She bit her lip.

"You don't have to tell me if you're not ready." *Why is he so nice? Why am I so at ease?*

"Nor do I have to go out with him until I'm ready," Justine thought about replacing the ring, instead she just rubbed her finger.

They finished breakfast without any more reveals.

XVI

Lenor's phone rang. "Hello."

"It's me," she knew Mac's voice

"Hi Theodore."

"What do you think about donating kidneys?"

XVII

There was a dinner break. Across the street was a fifties style diner. Urban and Duchane decided to go there. The specials menu was reasonable. Hal got a club sandwich and a chocolate shake. Justine got steak and eggs and water. "I swear you have a tapeworm," she quipped.

"There are worse reasons to be scrawny." He took a sip and got whipped cream on his nose. They shared a laugh as he wiped it off. This awkward young man now knew more about Justine than anyone at the paper.

"Can I straight with you?" Her eyes were tired but still haunting.

Haven't you been? was his first thought but Urban philosophized instead, "If you are going to be a successful stateswoman than I hope you are always straight when you talk, all the time no matter what." The writer was well read and the more sober he was the more he remembered what he had read in the past. It amazed him.

"I'm serious Horatio," Duchane barked.

"Please tell me what's on your mind," he made a little waive arm bow over the table. She started and stopped. "It's okay."

"No, I mean it *is* okay. But I don't open up like this with every man I meet or any man I meet, or any woman for that matter. I don't know why I'm talking so much," Justine had amazed herself and him.

"And I'm grateful," was all the writer could think to say. "I've opened up you."

"Thank you." The politician bit her lip. "So I think it's only fair to you that I tell you that can't run for town council."

"I," now he bit his lip.

They stopped talking.

They didn't speak through the late showing. They didn't speak on the way back to the B and B.

Justine had thrown a wrench into a good weekend.

And she knew it.

Damn.

The conversation had stopped.

She had broken the deal.

She had also put her ring back on.

Forget the EMT.

 She went to her door and Hal to his.

"So," Hal began.

"So," Duchane agreed. "Are you going to some writing?"

"I,"--now he hesitated again. This time he lied. "Sure."

"Okay then." They went in. He sat on the bed staring at beige curtains on closed window. Justine Anabeth Duchane went to the open adjoining door. "Good night." He didn't respond. She locked it.

Half an hour later she knocked on the door. "Hey Urban!" No response. Taking initiative, the political theorist opened the door. Light off, TV off. Room empty. *Damn.* Bathroom empty. *Damn.* She got her shoes.

She had a guess. They had passed a building two doors down. Not knowing why, Justine ran to

Kelly's Irish Ale, on the other side of the theater. Horatio Albert Urban was holding three fingers of whiskey. *"Lethe."*

"Don't drink that Hal." She sat on the barstool next to him.

"You get to hide I get to hide." *Time to put my money where mouth is.* "Stupid pipe dream." He started to pick up the glass and she put her hand on it.

Then Justine put a pen from his room in front of Urban, "Two club sodas," she told the bartender. Then she took the ring off and dropped it in his drink.

"Don't bullshit me," he stared at the sinking fake diamond.

"Horatio, you trade John Barleycorn for a cup of club soda and I'll throw my hat in for the town council on Monday." The bartender put the nonalcoholic drinks down and watched them. He was big and handsome and reminded them of Pierce Brosnan. They ignored him, Urban stared at the glasses. "I promise." He picked up a club soda. So did she. "You have some writing to do. I'm reading everything you've written in an hour."

"Deal." They clinked glasses.

XVIII

Pam broke. Did she have something better to do than shoot pool with her EMT partner? No. She sunk not one but two solids went in. "Damn." Benson stood against the wall under a beer sign, leaning on his pool cue. "How in hell did you do that?" Was all the befuddled man could say.

"I'm good." The Pocket skirted the line between clean and dirty. A few people shot darts. Three of the four pool tables were now in use. They were not the only EMTs, firemen or policemen in the bar. It was a hangout. It was a fun place to shoot pool.

Tyler scratched. "Paul Newman you ain't." The big man laughed out loud. The small woman gave him a blank stare. "The guy who taught Tom Cruise to shoot pool."

Recognition dawned slowly. "Oh," Pam said slowly. He got the cue ball and knocked in a stripe. "Not bad for someone collecting social security."

She was sassing him. He answered with another stripe. "Whatever," laughing he pointed with the cue. "Corner pocket." He sunk it.

"Not bad for a geezer." They laughed. That was high praise from a hustler like her.

"Shut up," he rim shotted the next ball.

"See, too old to compete." They eyed the table.

"I got this one," a cute tall blonde waitress in jeans and Yankees Jersey, number 23, came over. She had empty green eyes. "Two Buds." She grinned at him.

"Okay Romeo," they watched the waitress walked away. "You win I flash you, I win you tongue kiss the waitress." Matt shook his head. "Chicken."

"No, if you flash me we get thrown out; if I tongue kiss the waitress we get thrown out." That was probably true. "Loser buys."

"Deal." He didn't get another turn. The waitress was serving when the eight ball fell. That's how fast it went.

XIX

There was a knock on the adjoining door. Then again, he didn't expect different. It was getting late. Hal barely looked up from the notebook, "come," he impersonated her favorite starship captain.

Justine found him in black sweats and old Rose Thorns t shirt, writing away. She wore her same clothes. She was barefoot. The writer was engrossed.

The words were almost there almost. "So I guess you've been writing."

"Deal's a deal," he didn't look up. "Here," he slid one notebook across the table and kept writing away.

"What do we have here?" The politician asked. "Bottom of the fourth? Divorce?"

"Plays don't get written in order," no story does.

Duchane read and Urban kept writing. "You've been doing your job and well." She crinkled her nose. "He's a bit bitter. You know pain."

The writer stopped and looked at her, leaning back, hands out palms up--pen on the table. "Doesn't everyone?" Then he thought better of himself. "Sorry."

"No it's fine. It's time to let go of Kurt, he's not all men." *In for a penny.*

"Maybe I should name a villain after him," they shared a wry smile.

"He wasn't a villain, just not good enough." Justine looked at the pad. "Nah, make him an evil bugger." They laughed.

"I'll take him from a very dark place." Hal scribbled a note. "Kick Kurt in the teeth." The politician snickered at that. "Bastard. Then again, aren't we all?"

"All men aren't bastards," Justine Anabeth Duchane corrected Horatio Albert Urban.

"Don't start that," he had lost all faith in his own gender a long long time ago. "Don't defend me." That made her frown.

"A bastard with no redeeming qualities wouldn't have those stitches," she gingerly touched his scalp. "Rare breed of courage."

The writer got up and started to pace. "I'm not a hero. I'm not John Wayne. I'm barely a writer." He was just a guy trying to write a play. Not Superman, not Rambo and not even Kyle Reese. "I'm not Crockett or Tubbs or something."

"You aren't that kind of hero," Duchane's voice crack and she sat on the bed. "But you are my friend and I don't make friends easily." They made eye contact and Urban got dizzy. This was a big deal. They didn't have many friends, certainly not like each other. They were too broken people. "Yes," as if she was realizing it herself. "You are my friend."

"I like that," he leaned over and shook her hand. "You too." It was not meant to be flirtatious.

"Kurt took more than my heart," and Hals's stomach sank. *Oh boy.* Now he was in it, up to his waist. *Shit.* "He took my last phone call."

"I was ready to be married. It was just three weeks before the wedding, He was pulling away. The writer already had the story in his head and he was scared. She moved closer. "I was half moved into his apartment. I had his key. I often slept at my friend Jess's apartment as well, she was my best friend--the sister I always wanted as opposed to my own sister."

"You had a confidant" Her ending. was in his head before she spoke.

"Well, my sister Kathryn and I grew together since then. We grew up but back that it was," Hal could predict it, "Jus and Jess." He opened and closed his mouth. Her tale to tell. "Kathryn was in college. She's younger and prettier."

"Oh come on," Urban interrupted, "Um sorry," he sat on the other end of the bed. "Please continue." She slid closer.

Duchane was cracking up. "That's another story." They had to stop laughing. It was not a happy story that she was telling. "I went to his apartment and found Jess with Kurt." That was a strong 'with.'

"Then they looked at you," Hal looked Justine in the eye, "and you lost the two most important people in your life and in that horrible moment they lost the most important person in their lives."

There was silence and the politician leaned closer to the writer. "Yes," she whispered and tried to kiss him gently. He moved away really fast.

"No." He pulled away. She reached for him.

"I'm not usually," he was standing up and backing away. "Hal it's okay, I feel...really good about this...about you." Thankfully she hadn't reached for her shirt.

"I can't." she lay on an elbow and raised an eyebrow. "We can't."

"I don't understand. We like each other and you find me attractive?" Maybe she had gone too far too fast and was making a mistake. *Damn.*

"Oh sex with you would be incredible but then Monday it would be over." She settled her brow. "We'd go back to being strangers and it'd be awkward." Justine sat up. "Or we could take the other option in the room tonight." She studied his face.

"What are you thinking?" He sat in one of the wooden chairs.

"We have started a friendship these last two days. Those things don't come along every day." That made Justine Anabeth Duchane think.

Horatio Albert Urban was right. "So we go home and keep doing what we'd been doing?" That was a good idea.

"Yes."

She smiled. "I agree. Let's not blow the friendship." She picked up the notebook she had dropped on the bed, "and this is too good to screw up."

"Real friendships don't come along every day," the politician grinned.

"No they don't." She stood up and went to her door.

"And there is man a back home you're interested in." How well he knew her. There was. Matt the big EMT. "But for the record," the writer smirked. Duchane stopped in the door.   "Yeah?"

"There's no way your sister is prettier." They cracked up.

"Shut up." It took a while to stop laughing.

XX

After he left the bar Benson went to Cannonville Beach. He parked in front of A and F Concessions that would open Memorial Day weekend. He walked between the dormant cannons that gave the town its name and the memorial stone to Molly Sanderson, the college girl who was killed by drug dealers in 1982. Her killers had been brought to justice. The big EMT was not worried about being on the beach this late for three reasons, he was big, he was an EMT and the crime had been eliminated. That's another story.

There were several cars with teenagers. He ignored them and walked out on the beach. He had his shoes on. He just liked to watch the moonlight on the water. This made the universe feel big and his problems feel small. The job was good, the friends were good and his health was good but somehow he felt empty.

At thirty-two, Matthew Jason Benson knew what was wrong. He was lonely. He wanted a family, wife, kids, house and dog. He was looking for something. It wasn't about sex, a guy that looked like him could always find sex. That's why dating in your twenties sucks; to say nothing of the Aids crisis. He wanted to find love.

SUNDAY

Justine woke to the sound of her alarm. There was a knock on the adjoining door. "Yeah," she sat up, holding the blanket over her sweat pant covered legs. She had a t shirt on. Hal opened it, in the same clothes she had last seen him in. He had two cups of coffee.

"Friends?"

She smiled and agreed. "Friends." Gratefully the politician accepted her coffee. "Thank you." He leaned on the door jam and sipped his. "When did you get up?"

"Yesterday. I wrote all night." Duchane knew she should scold him but she grinned.

"Did you find the words you needed?" Urban nodded.

"Yes." He gestured to the now neatly stacked notebooks. "I'm happy with it. I can type it at home when I'm not working on your campaign."

"Good and I'm feeling really fulfilled, you were right." They shared a smile.

"Thank you," he didn't move.

"I know this is a clique," it took a moment, "Hal, do you have someone to call every night?" He grinned. "Now that you're sober?"

"Nope." As she had fallen asleep, Justine Anabeth Duchane had made a decision.

"Now you do." Horatio Albert Urban grinned.

XXI

The Cannonville Playhouse was not a movie theater and as far as anyone under forty was concerned it had never shown a movie. It had up until *Gone with the Wind.* It was a converted barn that been converted into a posh climate controlled luxury theater. They had gone from straw hat summer stock to play time of the rich in one generation. Seats ranged from twenty to two hundred dollars a pop in 1988. It was *the* place to be and many actors you've seen on TV have performed there.

It was a Spring with Shakespeare. Hal had seen the *Hamlet* production. He never missed *Hamlet.* A kid who couldn't make up his mind, it rang with Hal. He was also named after The Dane's best good friend a stagehand had been injured in an accident and could not be moved. He had been building the boat for *The Tempest.* So 911 was called. Guess who got the call? That's right. Everyone's favorite two EMTs Matthew Jason Benson and Pamela Suzzette Tyler. "Every see a play here?"

Matt laughed and parked. "Nah, I was a jock, remember." He was a football star, not a theater type. Another thing he didn't get.

"I was techie in high school," he looked blank. "A stagehand," Tyler went on. "When Cannonville High school auditorium was renovated my junior year, I got to use this stage. We performed the Scottish Play here. It was an experience."

"Scottish Play?" Benson was confused. "Hamlet?" The little EMT laughed.

"No silly, that's Danish. You know. 'There's something rotten in the state of Denmark?" She giggled. He opened the doors.

"Oh, you mean Macb," —his partner jumped.

"Shut your mouth!" He did.

"What?" She jumped out of the ambulance.

"Come out here now!" Matt didn't move.

"Pam, seriously," —Tyler put her hands on her hips, indignant.

"Seriously, Matt." He jumped down.

"You're being crazy, we have a bleeding patient," —not being nerd he didn't get it.

"Spin around three times and spit," the fiery little woman barked.

"Now Pamela Suzzette Tyler, this is getting out of hand." There was steam coming out of her ears.

"Spin!" He spun. Three full terms.

"Now spit!" He didn't. The parking lot was empty.

"Pamela?" She waited.

"Spit damn it!" He spat.

"What?" Tyler wiped her brow.

"Whew that was close," she leaned on ambulance. "Too close."

"What was?" Benson was thoroughly confused.

"Everything." She reached for the gurney. "You can't say that word in a theater or on the grounds. It's bad luck."

"You don't really believe that?" They opened the gurney.

"Of course I do." He reached his long arms for the gear.

"Superstitious claptrap." Matt slammed the doors.

"You kneel to a cracker," Tyler reminded her friend.

"I wouldn't put it like that." Benson slammed the doors.

"Neither would I." They started walking. "You have your beliefs and I have mine."

"You're right," he thought about that. "You're right I'm sorry."

"You should meet Carolyn's boyfriend Chuck, he's a professional actor. He's really superstitious, same dinner every night before a performance, without fail." That really shocked the big EMT but not he didn't go there.

"Your sister Carolyn?" He thought back. They hadn't met. She lived upstate.

"Yes sir," they passed the dilapidated rock garden that was close to being remodeled into a five-star restaurant. They opened the doors to climate controlled converted barn.

There was a poster next to the door. They were also running ads:

Oberon Community Newspapers, A and F Inc. & Pennyless Video

Present

Cannonville Playhouse's

Annual

New Playwrights Contest

Invitation to new unpublished material

For consideration

Grand Prize

10,000 and a two-week run

Possible Tour available.

XXII

The last movie on the docket was *The Portrait of Jenny*. Horatio Albert Urban, flopped back in his seat he was amazed that Justine loved the oldies as much as he did. At the climactic tear-jerking ending that had once bankrupted David O Selznick, the politician cried. She thought of Matt.

The screen changed to the eponymous painting and it went to color. "Most men never would have done that." The writer just stared at Jennifer Jones' image.

The other, shorter, owner appeared in front of the darkening screen as the lights came up. She also wore the red vintage suit. Hal disliked these parts. "Producer David O. Selznick kept that painting of then wife Jennifer…" she droned on.

"Ready?" He asked. The politician's answer was to stand and follow him out.

"I have to tell you Urban, I've never been to classic movie festival before, it was tremendous fun," she spoke in the lobby." He walked on.

"Diner one last time?" Hal asked.

"Sure." She held the door for him and they looked both ways. Same frumpy waitress with iron grey hair and same truckers at the counter not to mention the same calls that 'orders were up'. They looked at their menus, "Joseph Cotten was in *Laura?*"

That was a classic Oscar nominated noir from the same period as the festival, but with a different actor. "Dana Andrews," the writer offered, "better looking cus."

The politician grinned, "you know, for an educated man you don't speak in, I, erm...your speech is not,"--suddenly she realized she didn't know how to put it.

"I don't speak elevated English," Horatio Albert Urban explained.

Their drinks were served. Yes, he had another shake. She had water with a twist of lemon.

"No, you sure don't."

"I hate pretentious pricks who feel they need to speak the King's English circa sixteen ten," even the waitress taking an order at the next table had to laugh at that.

"You certainly blend in," Justine rolled her eyes and looked at a happy couple on the other side of the room, a bit jealous.

He leaned back and put his hands out, palms up, grinning. "Does it bother you?" *Amazing how much more fun life is sober.*

"Not at all," she shook her head at her friend's nuances. He wasn't a total dude and wasn't dying of testosterone poisoning like Book Booker.

"I suppose you and I have a different outlook on life than we did last Tuesday afternoon," even for a playwright he waxed poetic for a moment.

That just made the politician think. "It's true and not in a bad way." She sipped her water and he slid his shake off the placemat. There was chess game in progress printed on the paper. "What?" He was studying it.

Hal traced his fingers on the mat and chuckled. "Checkmate in six movies." That made his friend laugh. She compared the mats, hers was the same.

"Hey, you doing anything after work Tuesday?" It came out as a mumble.

"You mean other than trying to find words in the cracks in the ceiling?" the writer asked, making a joke about it.

"If I give you my address do you want to bring Chinese and show me how you can win a chess game in less than seven moves?" He just grinned

"Why not?" Their waitress came and they ordered some light dinner, literally soup and salad. Simple and light driving food.

"Maybe it is time," Justine bit her lip, "that I go back and ask that guy out."

Hal's eyes lit up. "Oh, do tell."

"I was hit on by the EMT that worked on your head," that made him think.

"The pretty girl who held a bandage on my head?" He was confused.

That made her laugh. "No, the big guy that looked like Napoleon Solo, he brought me flowers at work the next afternoon."

"Nap,--I must've been hit on the head harder than I thought, I don't remember *The Man from Uncle* showing up. Was David McCallum there too?" The writer tried to think back.

"What?" They chuckled. The politician rubbed the pale white circle where her ring used to be. "Matt was as bold as brass, I shot him down, but you know it was romantic."

"Ilya K,"--Hal was hung up on this, afraid he'd missed a celebrity.

"No, *Matt*, the EMT, he just looks like a young Robert Vaughn." They laughed.

"Oh." He got it. "Do you know how to locate him?" Urban knew she'd find him.

Justine thought, eyes up to the side. "I suppose I'll walk up to the fire station."

MONDAY

Matthew Jason Benson was cleaning the outside of ambulance while Pamela Suzette Tyler was doing inventory. They were in uniform. "Double count those gauze packets."

"I did," she lied and then obeyed. He just grinned, standing and bending to dip the sponge in a red firehouse bucket.

As the garage door was open, anyone could just walk in. "Hello," a female voice cracked.

Benson dropped the sponge. Tyler had to duck into the passenger seat to not interrupt with her laughter. Justine carried two gas station coffee cups. "Well, I guess there are second chances," Pam spoke between laughs.

"Hot chocolate?" He stood there befuddled. "Hello Matt, how are you today?"

"Um, you brought hot chocolate?" He was slow on the uptake.

The passenger door of the ambulance opened, almost knocking him over. "Give me the cocoa, you take her on a date," Tyler called out.

The older two laughed. "Please," the politician walked closer, "have one," she held them both out. Tyler snagged one. Benson just stood there befuddled.

"Yes, he'll go out with you, he's just slow." The two women looked at each other. "I'm Pam Tyler, junior EMT, no competition." She shut the door.

"So," the big man spoke slowly.

"I was hoping," Justine held out the drink again and he took it, "that offer for dinner was still open." She shifted her weight from one foot to the other in her blue flats.

"That would be great." She pulled a business card from her pocket and a pen.

Then she scribbled on it. "Here's my number."

"Thanks," he accepted it. "How about tonight? I'm off at,"--he had blanked.

"Two, you idiot," a voice called from inside the ambulance. They laughed.

"I guess I'm free," Matt agreed.

Justine thought for a moment. "I guess so. Luigi's at five thirty?"

He hesitated. Something was in his eyes. "That would be...good."

"I'll see you then," she smiled and walked away. He watched befuddled. She turned onto River Street and disappeared Benson had a date! *That was new,* Pam thought to herself.

Benson put down the drink, pocketed the number and picked up the sponge. "Wow."

"You're welcome." Then small EMT came out of the ambulance.

"That was a bit much, even for you," she was laughing.

"Oh come on, you're just embarrassed Matt," Tyler leaned against the vehicle and sipped the hot chocolate. "I did get you a date."

"*You* got me a date?" he splashed her with the wet sponge. "You, you," —

Pam was squealing. "Benson, Benson, Benson. I saved your sorry butt with that girl." He splashed her again. She went for the bucket.

"Alright!" Jeremy's voice boomed from the top of the fire pole. "Back to work!"

"Yessir," the small woman saluted.

"Sorry boss," the big man hopped to.

"Ah, forget it." Their captain went back to whatever he had been doing.

"Matt's got a girlfriend," the small EMT mocked

"Shut up Pam," the big EMT barked.

"I'm having fun," she giggled and got back in the ambulance. "I'm glad she came back. She seems to be a good one."

XXIII

Justine Anabeth Duchane leaned back from her typewriter and stretched. 4:45 PM. She rubbed each wrist. "I've got something for you," a voice spoke to her.

The politician looked to see Horatio Albert Urban with some legal papers. "Already?"

"Book and I took a ride at lunch," he didn't say he had to buy lunch for the ride, "I picked these up at town hall."

"Are those what I think they are?" Justine asked, surprised at his speed and diligence.

"As requested, signature forms and all the forms you need to fill out to enter the race for the November." The little writer held them out and the politician, who gratefully accepted them smiling. He also had clipboards.

"Thank you," she leafed through them.

"Give me what I need and Book and I will hit up the Walbaum's parking lot tonight getting signatures." She started writing the head of those forms. "I'll make myself a complete nuisance until they're full."

"This is really sweet of you," was all she could say.

"Justine, you stopped me from doing something really stupid and I'm most of the way through a rough draft of a great play. Things are looking up and this," he accepted the first sheets back, "this will be a fun distraction,"

"And Book?" It was no secret that he'd need a ride. "What about him?"

"He'll never turn down a chance to meet girls." Kelli Jones walked up to them in green flip flops and matching dress.

"I'm confused, what happened to the hot EMT?" She looked disapprovingly at Hal.   "Oh, I'm running for town council," the bubbly blonde's mouth dropped open, "mister Urban here is campaigning for me."

"Oh," Kelli looked between them, eyes widened. "Oh." She was confused. "Wait, what?"

"I'm throwing my hat in for politics, it's time to stop hiding," the politician explained.

"Hiding from what?" Justine handed the last set to the writer.

"That's all Hal, just bring them to me in the morning, or when their full, okay?" He nodded and clipped them to his clipboards.

"I'm running for town council," the politician spoke slowly. They could hear Lenor locking up, "he is getting signatures. This town needs good conservative leadership."

The writer turned to go. "Now that's a cause I can get behind," the older woman approached, ebullient. "Hold on Hal." He stopped. "I'm signing first." He came back.

"Okay." They looked at her. She signed under Justine's signature. "Okay Urban, what have you been up to?"

"He's been writing a play, a good one," Duchane interjected.

"That's what you went to college for. That's great!," they all looked at her. "What? I've read all your resumes." Whatley patted his cheek maternally, "Now, you and Book go fill these pages up."

"Night," Horatio Albert Urban nodded at his candidate.

He then obeyed and left. "Thanks Lenor," Justine began. "Hey, where was Mac?"

"He's," Whatley was not ready to say 'in counseling,' so she improvised, "taking some time off. Improving himself."

"What about tweedle dee and tweedle dum?" Jones asked.

"Oh, the bobsey twins?" They looked at the darkened office. "He let me fire them."

"That's great Miss Whatley." The bubbly girl didn't know what to say. "Will he leave us alone?" That's all then women at the paper cared about.

She sighed. "Yes," was the answer after a long time.

"Justine has to go get ready, she has a date with that hot EMT," the politician put her hands on hips. Lenor laughed.

"Now, this day is going *very* well," Whatley grinned.

XXIV

"Justine Duchane, masters in poli sci is running town council, all I'm asking is to give her a chance to run, this is not a vote." By the thirtieth or fortieth request Horatio Albert Urban was answering questions before they were asked. Only half the people said yes and it was taking time but the reactions were getting entertaining.

"Is she a republican or a democrat?" A wealthy woman pushing a shopping cart full of the most expensive things asked. "Or independent?"

"She's a friend and I'm not asking for your vote," yet, "just permission to run." The woman kept pushing her cart, her boots were worth more than Justine's car.

"I would only sign if she were a democrat," the tanned woman said, "have to be in solidarity with the women and blacks."

"I'm a woman," another voice came from behind them. "What about my right and my black husband's right to efficient government and low taxes."

They turned to see Dr. Liz Burma in brown slacks, black shoes and a white sweater. "I don't know," the first woman walked away.

"What about you, flyboy?" The medical woman asked the writer.

"Oh, I just want to give my friend a chance to win the election." Her maternal gauze appeared and she smiled.

"Are you writing?" Urban smiled there in the grocery store parking lot. "Give me the pen." She signed with a grin.

"So who is Justine Duchane?" Burma asked. By the way, her husband Mark is of color, but they only brought it up when someone said that republicans didn't care about blacks. Mark Burma's family had been republicans since President Grant was elected.

"A friend from work," he gratefully accepted the clipboard back

"Is she a good republican?" he shrugged.

"You ever read *Decline of the American Empire*?" The doctor laughed. "That's her."

"Pen name?" He nodded. "She's got my vote. How many signatures do you have?" He looked at Booker who held up his open hand twice.

Hal counted his page. "About fifteen."

"I'll walk with you," she smiled maternally. "We can call my husband at the payphone and he'll bring some friends by." They walked towards the phone. "So how's the writing?"

"Almost a complete rough draft…"

XXV

The politician was late and no one cared. She hadn't changed or even put deodorant on, the EMT was waiting in front of the one step up to the door of Luigi's Restaurant across from the train station, just south of the firehouse. She had driven her car and parked almost in front of him. He was wearing a green sweater and cords, black shoes. He had not brought flowers, had thought about it and then thought the better of it.

"Hi," Justine bit her lip nervously.

"I made reservations." It was a reasonably priced in vogue restaurant that served Italian and American food. "I bussed tables here in high school." He opened the door for her.

"I like the food," Justine spoke, surprised to have butterflies in her stomach like a silly teenager. She had eaten the top sirloin once or twice at Luigi's place.

"You look lovely," there were many people, business folks and others waiting. There was a dividing wall almost in front of them, to the right was the main of three dining rooms and to the left was a full bar that was standing room only.

"Um," she didn't want to be cliqued.

"Hope you're not a vegetarian," that made her laugh and saved the mood.

"Hell no," the politician chuckled, "carnivorous in every way." He waved to a big man with grey hair across the bar area.

"Well good, I'm a prime rib man," she pretended to giggle.

"Ooh, prime rib," she put on a faux ditz, "do I sound like a cheesy blonde?"

The Yankee game was on and as it was 1988 they were probably losing. The late eighties was not a good time for the Yankees. A uniformed cop appeared from the crowd, she looked familiar to Duchane. "Benson." The cop patted his back.

"Sully." The name tag read Sullivan Hastings. He looked at his date. "You've met Justine." *How could I forget?*

"Oh yes," they shook hands. "I saw you guys from the back and wanted to say 'hi.' Tom," her husband, "and I are eating with Detective Conrad," Rose PD, "his wife, mayor Meylor," Rose, not Cannonville, "and her husband."

"I don't want you to keep them waiting." Justine was a bit in awe. Lady Cop pumped the politician's hand.

"You be nice to this guy, he's one of the good ones," and Sully walked away.

"Wow," the politician whispered.

The grey haired man was upon them "Matthew."

"Tony," they shook. "Justine, this is Anthony Berra, my old boss." The co-owner's hand made her hand look a baby's hand as he accepted it and the Old Italian American kissed it.

"A pleasure, any friend of Matthew's." He waved to a busboy standing in a doorway to the side and more intimate dining room, "Jorge, make sure Matthew and his lady friend make it to their table." He patted the EMT's shoulder. "Drinks are on me; Paulo will take care of you." He turned to a customer who wanted his attention.

"Thank you," the dates said together but he wasn't listening, the work was never done. There was a shelf of caricature statues over the bar, eighty years of pop culture icons from WC Fields to a modern Reagan, not the actor Reagan.

"Yes boss," the busboy was early twenties, mustached and wore a plain white shirt with black pants--the uniform, "Please," he gestured toward the doorway.

"Course," Benson patted Jorge's back. "Good to see you."

"You too," he tapped a chalkboard on the way. "Specials, same place as always. May I get your drink order for Paulo?" He asked, gesturing to a small man, serving a tray, with the look of a tv actor, blonde hair, flawless skin, women loved looking at Paulo Giovanni.

It was a busy restaurant. "So," they sat. Matthew Jason Benson looked up. "Beer, same as always." Coors.

"White wine, house is fine," Justine Anabeth Duchane agreed and Jorge walked away.

"So," Matt said again. "Do you have a boyfriend?" He asked.

She leaned forward and whispered. "Would I be here?"

"It's just," the big EMT's voice cracked. "The guy in the with the bump on his head."

She cracked up. "Oh Hal." It took a while to settle down. several couples looked at them. "He's just a friend. Maybe a political ally, that's all…"

"Oh…" There was a question on the tip of his tongue.

"What about you?" Benson looked blank.

"Huh?"

"Girlfriend?" He shook his head. "As popular as you are."

Now Matt was even more confused. "What?"

"Police captain, Rose mayor," Meylor was a democrat, "owner of the top restaurant in town. Who aren't you friends with?" Was that a blush on the big man's face?

"Well in my line of work you see a lot of police and fire types." He really didn't know what to say. He hadn't thought about it.

"And Tony?" The giant teddy bear of an Etruscan. Justine leaned down, more interested.

"Oh, he and my dad were good friends. He gave me a job in high school. He also came to all my football games. I worked hard and we got along well." Benson explained, "he has a business partner that works the books, Luigi. They've been at this since the sixties.

"Luigi's Place?" That was the full name, no one ever said it.

"Drinks," Paulo appeared. "Hey Benson."

"PG." Coworker humor, you have to be there. It's a secret where that nickname came from and I don't know it.

"Good to see you." They watched the little white squares and drinks touch the table. Then two waters, "Do you want to hear the specials?" He put the tray under his arm.

"I'm good." Duchane smiled.

"So am I," her date agreed.

"Prime rib, rare, baked potato and Italian on my salad." She tried now to sound rehearsed. The girls in her family knew what they liked.

Grinning Matt looked at the waiter. "Prime rib, well done, spaghetti and I'll have the minestrone instead of the salad." Again, he showed that this place was a second home.

"Cool. Jorge will bring bread," he walked away.

"Okay, this is your place," Justine grinned.

"No, it's Luigi's. Tony was an accidental partner. Luigi was going to go into business with Paulo's dad but the old man couldn't come up the money. They had another name," he paused, "no one can remember it. Anyway Luigi was pressed for time and Tony borrowed the money from his mother and saved the day."

"And Paulo's dad?" Ever the politician, she had to ask.

"In the kitchen from day one. Still friends." He shrugged those big shoulders.

"Makes sense, it's just seemed that when we walked in you were a local legend, everybody knew you," where had she heard that before. Matt laughed. "It's your *Cheers*?"

"Maybe," he stammered.

Tony Berra himself brought the bread. "Don't order the Tony's Special Chicken, it's crap," the big Italian American joked and put two plates and butter down as well. He took the menus making a tsk tsk sound. "I'm so happy to meet you Justine. You are the first girl that Matthew has ever brought in for dinner." *No wonder he had hesitated.* A tray was dropped in the back dining room and plates shattered. "Damn, excuse me," the owner started to walk away. "Uneasy lies the head…" he disappeared swearing in Italian.

"*Never* brought a girl here?" Now Duchane almost blushed.

"Well, Pam and I have drank here, all the EMTs drink here. It's kind of a thing; even the ones who have sodas at tables and not beers at the bar." He sighed. "Tradition is that the crew gets together and buys the junior EMTs their first beers here for their twenty-first."

"This *is* your special place." Duchane observed, knowing the answer. *Maybe Hal's right and I am a born politician.*

"It is," Benson looked embarrassed. "I guess it is, I mean…" he hadn't realized it completely or how uncomfortable he'd feel until this moment. *Shoulda trusted my gut.*

"I'm honored," she lied, feeling uncomfortable as well.

"Hey," Paulo saved them from the moment. "Tony said *all* your drinks, even refills are on him." Justine gave him a smile.

"PG, this is Justine," they shook hands.

"Sir?" A matronly woman called the waiter.

"Scuse me," he left.

The two people looked at each other. "I'm sorry Justine. I should have suggested anywhere else. This place is...well it's so special for me it's not a good place for a first date."

Justine Anabeth Duchane thought for a moment and Matthew Jason Benson studied her eyes. Again he was struck by that mixture of pain and confusion, though more muted. *That's a wound I'd like to patch up.*

"It's a restaurant and a good one. Let's enjoy it and not dwell," she said the words trying to make herself believe it.

"Hey, how is Hal your political ally?" He changed the subject. *Good catch.*

"Oh, I'm running for town council." That was news. "He's my campaign manager."

"Well, I'll campaign of you. Rose or Cann--oh that was a stupid question Rose is a city." They chuckled. "I live in Rose but I will campaign for you."

"You don't know what I stand for." Now it was Benson's turn to laugh.

"*The Decline of the American Empire* is pretty clear." She waited. "The receptionist told me." He had picked up that much.

"It's supposed to be a secret," she was a bit annoyed, "I get death threats you know."

"Well," Matt gave her an evil grin, "I gave her the smolder."

PART TWO
Two months in Summer

We walk in two shoes.

But we all want to live in one

Because when the other drops

That is when the journey starts

1988

June

The typewriter clacked:

IRA: SO THAT'S IT. IT'S OVER?

LOU: THAT PART.

IRA: WHY'D IT TAKE ALMOST NINETY YEARS TO FIGURE IT OUT?

LOU: SOMETIMES IT DOES, BUT YOU MADE GOOD IN **THE END.**

I

Horatio Albert Urban pulled the paper out of the typewriter and tapped the pages on his clean desk. *Mister Karlson would be proud.* He had bolded the last two words for effect and for that Mr. Karlson would not be proud. But it was done, for the first time since college fully typed, edited final draft of a quality play. There were two more outlines waiting.

"Nine Innings of Life." Hal smiled to himself and put it down, reaching for the phone. He was stone sober. He had been for two months. It felt good. The stitches were about ready to come out--well they had been, he'd been busy. He was even looking forward to that.

"Go for Booker," the velvety voice answered the phone. Hal grinned.

"Bertram, I'm sorry," the writer spoke seriously and sipped his water.

"Shhhh, don't call me that, I'm with a lady," the sound of a giggling blonde on the other side of the couch could be heard through the handset.

"Sorry to interrupt, I'm just in a really good mood and Justine's out with Matt," usually, Book had noticed, the last couple months it was she whom his friend called and Duchane called Urban. In fact, the heir to Billy Dee had noticed the two new friends, though not dating, were inseparable, if not together they were on the phone.

"Good job man, now I have a lady who likes baseball who wants to kiss me." Hal didn't want to know.

"I finished the play," the writer just had to say it.

"Good job," that his friend didn't get.

"Why do you put up with me?" That was a stupid question or so he had told Justine when she had asked him the same about Book over chess.

"Why shouldn't I?" That was a good answer and his ultimate answer.

"I appreciate it," okay now it was getting think.

"Horatio, I get it." They hung up the phone.

The writer took the manuscript to his bed. One more read through couldn't hurt. He was about at intermission when his phone rang. Hal got up and stretched on the way back to the phone on the desk. "Hello."

"Hal." It was Justine. He told her. "Finally." Laughter.

"Hey." He looked at the clock. It was about that time. The last phone call of the night.

"I had a really good time. *Crocodile Dundee II* wasn't bad. Coffee and donuts was better." She sighed. *So this is it? Girl talk.* He actually kind of liked it.

"That's great," it wasn't sarcastic. He meant it.

"You know; after almost two months he still gives me butterflies." Urban laughed

"Isn't that a real good thing?" Duchane giggled.

"I guess so. How well you understand me." They chuckled.

"Just trying to be a friend." He could almost hear her smile. Then the yawn was audible.

"Good night Horatio Albert Urban." That made the writer grin.

"Good night Justine Anabeth Duchane." The politician went to sleep smiling.

II

The next morning Justine should have been working and so should the big EMT on the other end of the line but they were chatting on the phone. The night before had been a really good date. Lenor Whatley, the only authority figure who what been in the office lately, liked the positive change in Duchane's demeanor and let it go.

"So maybe Friday we can invite some friends like Pam and Hal or whoever and get together at my place and watch *Ghost Story*," a great horror movie with Fred Astaire.

You can rent it at Pennyless Video. Hey! I'm just sayin.'

"Do you have it?" Matt asked.

"Yes, I have it tape in the townhouse." She was twirling the phone cord like she did in high school. It was not conscious gesture.

"Well, that sounds like a plan to me." He chuckled. "I saw that in the theater." He shuddered. "That actually scared me." It came out in 1981.

"Did you have fun last night?" She heard him smile.

"Yes. Yes I did. It was great." Justine leaned back in her chair. "And you?"

"Don't I always with you?" Lenor saw all this and smiled.

"And I with you," *Ahh, young love;* Whatley thought to yourself.

"You know what this may be?" Duchane whispered.

"Couplehood?" Benson whispered back.

"Well shucks, I haven't had that since…" her feet hit the ground.

"Justine Anabeth Duchane, this...this is us. This is new, I won't do to you what Kurt did you. I promise you that." He was right of course. It was just saying the words was hard.

"Hey it's not your fault Kurt was a loser," That's what she needed to say.

"I know, but as Hal is always saying, I apologize on behalf of my gender for all those losers." But you know. That word was too good

"You know what? Worse than a loser. He could hold a job and made good money," she corrected herself. "He was not someone to be trusted. He could not be faithful."

"It's better you found that out before you made it down the aisle." That was true.

"You're not that kind of man Matt." That was true.

"Justine, you what I've learned in my thirty-two years, as clichéd as it is?" She laughed.

"There's no innocent bystanders in love?" She waited.

"Love can cause you nothing but pain but it can also cause you nothing but joy, it all depends on what side you're on." He was right.

"What side are we on?"

"The right one." He hoped. BEEP. *Shit.* "Hey, my call waiting's going off."

"Talk to you soon." Click

She looked at the clock and dialed another number. "Sports," Hal picked up the phone. Half a baloney sandwich was on his left, manuscript on the right. He had about twenty minutes left on lunch.

"The package has been picked up." They laughed.

"Congratulations candidate Duchane." She had picked up a copy of the ballot. She was on it. Funny, she hadn't told Matt.

"Did you register the treasurer?" he asked.

"Um, Kelli did. You need to be a resident." They had gone over this several times. Kelli Jones of Jonathan Ln., off Treadwell. District 2. She lived in an in-law apartment within walking distance. She even could pass milk vending machines on the way home from work. It was convenient.

"You did Justine." Urban sipped his soda.

"We did it." Some soda came out his nose.

"You got me this far." He shrugged. She knew, she always knew. "Are you shrugging?"

"I'll get you elected too. That's how the story ends." Horatio Albert Urban was sure.

"Oh, I got you a pamphlet from the Cannonville Playhouse, I think you may find this contest interesting." He heard her sipping something.

"Contest?" She laughed.

"I'm going to see you get staged Horatio."

III

Matthew Jason Benson had double and triple checked the order. Justine Anabeth Duchane was *very* specific on the phone about her Chinese food. She was quite specific about...well everything. He didn't mind getting her order right. After all, that he was only seventeen minutes late. She opened the door to her townhome. She wore a cream short sleeved shirt and loose jeans. She was barefoot and her hair was pulled back. He wore a white t shirt and tight jeans with black sneakers.

"General Chang's Chinese takeout for mizzy Dutch-ane," Matt put on his worse Chinese accent but it succeeded in making Justine laugh.

"So, sorry," she continued the politically incorrect humor and looked his two full hands, food in paper bags with handles. "No cash-ee, must pay you in kisses."

As her date grinned his date leaned in and kissed him and then moved out of the way. He walked past his date, "Coffee table?"

The politician had laid out plates, utensils, coasters and paper towels. OCD? Just a bit. There was cans of soda in one of the bags. It was a large living area. She had signed the lease when she thought that she'd be sharing with Kurt and just stayed. "Yeah."

Benson was always amazed at how clean-- impossibly clean she kept it. On the kitchen/dining room table there was a chessboard, already set up. "Still trying to teach me chess?" After the movie.

"Yes, after we eat and watch the video." There was a Pennyless Video case on the TV. It held *The Searchers*, she was also trying to make him a John

Wayne fan. That was working. But he was still a democrat. Nobody's perfect.

Duchane began to serve. Another thing she had to do herself, God forbid something got spilled. "I'll start the movie." He tried not to watch her open and spoon food, it was a quirk that did get under his skin. *At least she has all her own teeth and no tattoos.*

Justine opened her soda and it sprayed all over her shirt. "Son of a bitch." Without thinking she pulled it off. Matt took a step back and averted his gauze. That was more of her than he'd seen yet.

"Erm…" Was that blush in his cheeks.

"Oh come on EMT, you've seen breasts before, you can handle my pink bra." She laughed and he stammered a chuckle. "Be right back." The politician turned and headed to the bedroom. Her boyfriend watched her go and enjoyed it.

"Alright." He studied the shadowy beginning in full Cinemascope on the television and plopped on the couch. "Marion Robert Morrison," the EMT snorted with laughter.

The politician joined her boyfriend wearing a George Strait t shirt. "Maybe I'll play some of him while we play chess," she gestured to the smiling cowboy.

"Well ma'am, that would be okay." That was a terrible southern as he watched her serve him and hold out the plate. "Thanks."

"Country okay?" He shrugged. "You are a country fan right?"

"Aren't we all?" Now Benson laughed.

"Good." She took her plate and began to eat.

"Second to Elton though." She smiled. "Mister Elton John will always be my favorite."

"He and Bernie Taupin," the lyricist, "are musical geniuses for sure, but there are plenty of musical geniuses out there. Country is the poetry of America."

Having no comeback Matt kept his mouth shut all through dinner. "I can do the dishes," was the next phrase out of his mouth.

"It's fine. I got it." Justine began to clear, patting her boyfriend's knee and abandoning him to John Wayne. He had to admit being served made him happy. She had to admit a clean apartment made her happy...so in that regard it was a win win.

"Maybe next time a love story?" The EMT asked.

"Sure, why not? I do have ovaries." The politician giggled. "It's just that too few movies can beat a real love story." That made our heroine sigh, "but I don't think those exist anymore."

Benson followed her with his eyes. "A real love story?"

"Well," she sat next to him and packed garbage into the paper bags. "Mom and dad have a really good one." She looked at her guest. "I'll leave these by the door, take them to the dumpster at the other end when you go, okay?"

The movie was ignored as the lady of the house talked. "Sure," Benson picked up the remote and lowered the volume. "Mom and dad?"

"They were pushing thirty when they met. "Dad felt he was too old for sport dating and he told so her over coffee. My father was auditioning for a wife." The look on Matt's face made Justine laugh.

"Uh-okay." He was lost.

"Mom told him she had been on date with an ex-boyfriend three months before, he was long gone and hadn't been heard from in a while. However, she had one reason why she'd fail her audition…" The voice trailed off and the hostess crossed her legs on the couch.

"Er," he had nothing. *Damn! Hal got it on the first guess.* Duchane tried not to crinkle her nose. The EMT waited patiently.

"She was late on her period and pregnant with my older brother." Benson's mouth dropped open.

"That must have been a big deal in sixty-five. Your dad just rolled with that?" Justine smiled. *Wow.*

"Dad is an awesome dad and an awesome father, there was never any doubt or question or word about it. In his eyes my brother is his son. Love beats blood every time." There was a distant look on her face.

"Daddy's girl?" That made her get a shit eating grin.

"Uh-huh." She picked up the remote.

"Hey, is his name on the birth record?" The politician put a finger to her his lips.

"Of course, now shhh. John Wayne." She turned the volume up. Benson leaned back and Duchane lay on his chest.

But later.

Hours later.

Three chess games, garbage in the dumpster, Matt gone home and dishes done later Justine made her last call of the night.

"Did I wake you?" She was in bed, in a long Snoopy nightgown.

"Writing another piece." Hal had been hard at work.

"I told him my parents' love story, I cut it short, he didn't get it." The writer stopped typing. That was sad.

"What's too get? He embraced your brother and surprised your mom on their third date with a ring box that had a note inside." *Are you busy on June 6th, 1965?* "I should put that in play." *Why?* "It would be more romantic than the crap on TV." *It's a good day to get married.*

"Just forty-eight hours." They grinned.

Thirty-three years and four kids later. Now that's a love story.

IV

It was lunch break and Duchane spent it on the bench outside the fire station eating sandwiches with Benson. "So how did you become Matthew Benson?"

He laughed. "You don't want to know."

She giggled. "Yeah, I do." It was a beautiful day. Pam was upstairs having work lunch, read corrective coaching with Jeremy.

"My great grandfather served in the Civil War. Private John Jason Benson." She waited. "He had a son many years later who died in World War One and his second son was a decorated war hero; Captain Lucas Jason Benson MD, don't ask. His son, my dad was in Korea, Lieutenant Mark Jason Benson. then came me. They kept the pattern."

"Pattern?" Her eyes opened wide. "No shit?"

"Matthew, Mark, Luke and John." He sighed. "I'm out of Gospels, if I ever have a son I guess we're on Paul." They laughed. "How'd you become Justine Anabeth?"

"Well, by great-grandfather was Julius Justice," he made a face. "I know, I lucked out. My great-grandmothers were Ann and Beth."

"Cute." He smiled. "And if you have a daughter?"

"What, with you?" The EMT looked away, embarrassed. "I'm playing." Was she? "Maureen Buttercup." He looked blank. "Well, Maureen O'Hara for the John Wayne side of my personality and Buttercup for *The Princess Bride.*"

"Why not Buttercup Maureen?" The politician shook her head.

"I'm far too old fashioned for that." Yes, we are all bundles of contradictions.

"Yeah, big families or small families?" She shook her head.

"No, you first." She wasn't going to be trapped.

"Two would be ideal." He was thinking about the possibility little Paul and little Maureen. He smiled. She wasn't thinking about it and didn't know why.

"Good size. What is your reasons?" Now she was trying to trap him.

"Well, I wouldn't cry at three but my dad always said the children should not outnumber the parents," that made Justine laugh. She rolled up the foil, wiped her mouth and put the garbage in the bag. He took his last bite.

I would like your dad Matt," he grinned, but the EMT always longed for a big family.

"He'd love you." She sighed.

"He's a liberal, isn't he?" The EMT shrugged.

"Devout Catholic, devout democrat from Boston stock. He has a picture of JFK in his living room." That made both of them laughed. "Oh, hey." He rolled up his garbage.

"What?" The politician watched him toss his trash to a metal barrel that was the firehouse's outdoor trash can and make the shot.

"Next Saturday I'm taking my sister's kid to the movies," the big EMT grinned. "Her name is Talia." Was he trying too hard or was he legitimately happy about it?

"Aww, you sound like a good uncle." He won some points.

"Well, I promised my sister." He took out his wallet and produced a photo of a cute little girl waving to the camera and held it out. "My brother-in-law is very Italian."

"I can see that and she's adorable." He replaced the picture. "She asked me for a cousin last year." The adults laughed nervously.

"Anyway, I have to work at six PM Saturday until six PM Sunday. Sunday is, unless..." the big EMT's voice trailed off.

"I'd love to come with you to the movie." Matt smiled at Justine's comment.

"That would be nice." He stood, happy. "Very nice."

"Kids are great." Nervously, the politician got up and walked to the trash can. "What's Sunday?" She was curious.

"Oh, one of Pam's...friend's has a reading at the Inkpot." It was a comedy club and poetry reading spot in Rose. Sunday was open mike night.

"Hmm. Poetry…" It was not her kind of place.

"It'll be angry and liberal," she giggled.

"I get it." Justine stretched. "An EMT night."

"Do you mind?" She just shook her head.

"Nah, I can call Hal and he can teach me new ways to beat you at chess." That made Benson laugh. "Not that I need help."

"No you don't." Duchane reached for Benson's chin and raised it. Then she kissed him.

"And you are a good boyfriend." She started to walk away. "Teachable."

"Teachable?" That was perplexing.

"No guy gets everything right on the first date." He sighed

"You said a big word." This time they weren't interrupted by call waiting. His girlfriend kept walking and looked over her shoulder.

"Shouldn't your girlfriend acknowledge it?" No joking and completely serious.

"Yeah." Watching her go he was confused.

"See you later." Matt watched her to the end of the street, looking both ways and crossing it and then until she was just a dot in the distance and sat down.

"Girlfriend." He had a big shit eating grin on his face. Then he punched the sky. "Oh yeah."

"What?" A fireman named Juan called from the open garage door. "She call you her boyfriend?" That was that.

V

Dr. Elizabeth Victoria Burma was reading charts of all the ED staff. She was a gregarious attending. A big likable gray haired orderly, in blue scrubs came up to her at the desk in the middle of the busy room. "There's a guy at the visitor's entry desk. He says that he has an envelope for you and if I give you his name you'll make time."

Liz looked up and rubbed her eyes. "What's his name?" Thirty-nine and getting too old for this shit. Next year the head of the ED was retiring and she'd go for it.

"Hal Urban?" The orderly looked blank. He saw so many patients roll in and out of the hospital he never remembered names.

The medicine woman stood up. "I'm on my way."

"Who is this guy?" Big Jim followed her, interested. He was between duties.

"A patient I took interest in." She stopped and held a hand out. "Now, no dirty thoughts. He's a writer with a drinking problem."

"Looks sober to be." A bedpan hit the floor and the orderly went to deal with it.

She continued and found Hal in clean jeans, clean black dress shirt that was tucked in and a new pair of white Converse. "Hello Doctor."

"Hello there, follow me." She gestured to the double doors. "Is that for me?" She opened the left door and received the package at the same time.

"One stageable play, already sent to theaters and publishers, flawlessly edited." Liz gave him a maternal grin.

"May I keep this?" He smiled.

"Absolutely." She wore pink scrubs under a white lab coat and led him through the ER to a free bed. "Should I?"

"Sit." He did and the doctor closed the curtain. Then Burma opened the envelope and thumbed it. "You kept up your end of the bargain." The papers were replaced.

"Thank you." The envelope landed on a counter and gloves were put on.

"Stitches coming out pro bono." She went to work.

"Hey, remember that petition you signed?" The medical woman did not look up. He could hear the snip snip sound.

"Justine Duchane, she's got my vote." He waited.

Finally, Hal spoke. "Got some phone lines, volunteers…"

"I can make calls." He grinned. "I can write a check too."

"Doc,"--

"Hey, I can donate to my party if I want to," snip snip. "So what's the play about?"

"Baseball and life." There was a long pause and the writer could feel the suture pulling from his head. It did not hurt but it was a weird feeling.

"I got that. Is it a comedy or a tragedy?" He told her. "Any leads on a theater?"

"Cannonville Playhouse has a contest." Urban could see the doctor smile.

"We have season tickets. My husband Mark is a real patron of arts."

"Don't you have to ask him before making out checks for obscure politicians?" Liz smiled. That was funny.

"I'll tell you two truths Hal," he waited. "First you know, I'm a doctor." He laughed out loud. "Hold still." Snip snip. "Second one is a secret," my sister whispered, "I make more than he does."

"That's great. I mean it really is." 1988, female doctor accomplishing that; Hal liked that.

"Tell me about Oberon Community Newspapers?" She was curious what had happened there and what they knew about Mac's change.

"Well, Mac Maguire, the editor is MIA. He left his administrative assistant Lenor in charge. Between you and me, she knows more about the business anyway. Actually the whole paper has been running smoother lately." He paused. "She donated from her own pocket to Justine's campaign. "Why?" He felt another stitch go.

"Mac, er--Theodore Roosevelt Maguire Junior was not the most popular boss?" Then Urban held his tongue. "Well, sometimes people change." She finished. "You'll be tender but you're all healed." She put a flashlight in his left and then right eye. "Sober too, excellent."

"People change?" He smiled. "I guess I did."

"Maybe you should look in room three twenty-one." She cleaned up and disposed of the biohazards. "There are surprises everywhere."

"Three twenty-one?" Liz picked up the envelope.

"I'll take you to the elevator." She did and he rode it up and then Hal followed several signs to several winding hallways--you know how hospitals are. He found an open door and then found Mac Maguire in a bed, reading a book on meditation.

The big man wore a hospital gown and looked smaller. "I hope I'm not disturbing you sir." Maguire smiled.

"No, please come in." The writer did and the editor put the book aside. "Just gave something up that someone needed more."

"Excuse me?" Hal was confused.

"Don't worry about me." Theodore Roosevelt Maguire Jr. smiled. "Dr. Liz said you would be up to see me sooner or later."

"I would?" The editor chuckled lightly and held his side.

"Justine Duchane is running for town council and she needs funds." Mac sipped his water. "She'd kill you if she knew you were here, so don't tell her."

"Sir?" Now Hal was really confused.

"Lenor has my new foundation's checkbook, I told her to anonymously donate anything the campaign needs." That shocked our hero.

"Why?" He waited and he watched the big man, almost pitiable in his new look, looking out the window. Either Mac was growing a beard or he hadn't shaved in a couple days.

"It's the right thing to do." He looked at Hal and smiled.

"Excuse me?" The little man almost fell over.

"I doubt she'll need as much as I can give." He motioned for the younger man to sit.

"As you say sir. Do you even vote?" There was another pained chuckle and the editor held his side again. Surgery? The writer was concerned.

"I'm not in her district but neither are you so who cares?" He finished his water and poured some more from the plastic pitcher. Urban sat.

"Thank you." The writer was at a loss for words.

"You're welcome." There a minute of silence. "How's your car?" He asked.

"Um...amazing," the price had strangely been lowered by about a grand when he finally went to pay for the repairs. "On time for work?"

"Yes sir." Now Urban was nervous.

"Well there's no way to ask this. Lenor says you wrote a play. She says you're giving your art a go, is that true?" There was a hesitation.

"Yes sir." What else could he say?

"I truly hope you succeed Hal." There was some coughing, Maguire looked weak. "Have you submitted it." Urban told him. "Really? The Playhouse?"

"Yes...um sir?" His voice cracked and there was more coughing. Mac took a sip.

"I'm sorry Hal, I need to be alone. I do wish you luck though." The writer got up to the sound of more coughing.

"Thank you, sir." He left and shut the door. That was not the Mac Maguire his employees knew. He was new.

Theodore Roosevelt Maguire Jr. waited for the pain in his throat to subside and then he sipped more water. The phone number he dialed on the hospital phone was memorized. "Cannonville Playhouse?" A woman answered.

"Kyle Coyt please," Coyt was the executive director and chief fundraiser. He had gotten plenty of money from Oberon Community Newspapers over the years.

"Who may I say is calling?" They knew the name. "Just one moment sire." *Sire*? He tried not to laugh. It hurt to laugh.

"Mac!" Maguire disliked Coyt immensely. Urban he respected.

"Coyt."

"What can I do for you?" The mealy mouthed little toad went on

"Did you read a play by Hal Urban?" There was a pause and some shuffling of papers.

"Yes. excellent play but he has a shit resume. I can't stage it." You don't say no to the owner of Oberon Community Newspapers--at least not in business.

"Why not?" There could be no good reason.

"The open slot wins ten grand. It should go to an established writer who can get picked up for a tour, he closes in two weeks and we get no royalties--'sides I can't sell out an unknown name." Mac sighed. It was audible and made Kyle uncomfortable.

"How do you know he won't?" The theater man got annoyed.

"It's his first play,"--stupidity annoyed Mac.

"Second, he staged in college." There was laughter. But only from Coyt.

"What you're serious? Maguire this is what I do." That was it. Time for hardball.

"My ten grand." That was mostly true.

"Oh come on,"--the executive was cut off.

"How much do you lose if it's *not* picked up?" Couldn't be back breaking.

"The royalties would come to…" some number crunching went on and Kyle padded it.

"I guarantee that and any seats you don't sell." He could afford it.

"The Playhouse will lose prestige," Mac sighed audibly.

"Let me make it simple. If *Nine Innings of Life* by Horatio Albert Urban is not staged, I withdraw my patronage up to and including the ten grand." Coyt dropped his phone. Finally, he returned still in shock.

"Are you okay Maguire?" That made Mac chuckle and hold his side.

"Never better. Look. You. Are. Doing. This. I. Am. Funding. It. *Capiche?*" Each word was said slowly and deliberately.

"You're insane but I guess I'm stuck, my other investors, Doyle and Clipper, can't or won't make up your portion and it's too late cancel the contest.

"I know." Winning a business negotiation felt good.

"You got my balls over a barrel." It hurt to laugh.

"I know." It felt good too.

"Why are you betting on this punk?" Though Kyle could not see him Mac shake his head. Horatio Albert Urban was no longer a punk. He'd earned it.

"I don't bet on losing horses, you know that. He'll sell out and get his run and he won't need any help from me to get that run. Just stage his play, the words will take the rest." The editor had won.

Now it was up to Hal.

"Have you even read it?" The door opened and Dr. Liz Burma walked in with a couple hundred Xeroxed pages and handed them to the editor.

"Holding it now."

VI

"I don't think I've ever seen you so happy," Pamela Suzette Tyler told Matt Benson as they pulled out of the hospital parking lot. He still wouldn't let her drive. "You've been ebullient."

"I gave her a necklace, she loved it." It was a lily shaped affair.

"Jewelry--yuck." Pam put her uniformed legs on the dashboard in disgust.

"She kissed me with tongue for the first time," usually he didn't share that type of information with friends, but Tyler was a girl--and that she'd get.

"Oooh, I'm down with that." She frowned. "Wait a minute. Two months and you haven't rung her bell yet?"

"There are more important ways to make a woman smile." The necklace was a present to celebrate their second month and titles. It was engraved on the back with Justine's initials. Matt was a romantic and Justine loved pink stargazer lilies.

"Ah," Pam rolled her eyes. So young, so not ready for life. "I can't think of one. Hell I've been a woman my whole life,"-- the senior EMT cut her off.

"Nothing leaves a more indelible impression than touching a woman's heart." He tapped his friend on the sternum. "Even you."

"Lame." He laughed.

"Well, Pammy, I don't tell you how to live your life, don't tell me how to live mine." He was both polite and adamant.

"I'm just telling you if you want to keep her, sooner or later you'll have to make an impression on another organ." Matt just kept laughing. "What?"

"What's the longest relationship you ever had? With anyone?" Tyler studied his face. "What do you remember best?"

"I dunno, weeks." She wasn't a commitment type. "I....don't remember." She looked blank. He had expected that.

"How's those stamps I gave you?" The little EMT smiled from ear to ear.

"I love 'em. They completed my set. I…hey!" She got it.

"Anything else touch your heart this year? Anything else you remember?" His friend looked out the window annoyed as he made a turn.

"I guess not. Why can't my sister meet a guy like you?" He sighed.

"We are out there." She shrugged.

"Anything else on that locket but her initials?" Matt shook his head.

"Nah, couldn't fit Elton lyrics on it." Pam rolled her eyes again.

"Is that more of that pop shit you listen to?" She asked. The big EMT shrugged. "It's slow, it's boring and it's sappy." He made another turn.

"It's deep and meaningful and tells a story," Benson countered.

"It's old and tired and my mom listens to it." Matt looked at Pam and Pam looked at Matt and they both cracked up.

"Well, she may be fifteen years older than me but she has great taste in music," that was his last word on that.

"Loser."

"Shallow," but they were laughing. Then she wasn't. He looked at her. "What?"

"You really think I'm shallow, I mean I'm slutty," she was frowning. "I might not believe in commitment," yet, "but shallow?"

That killed the mood. "No, Pamela, I didn't say it like that… I didn't mean,"--

A big grin covered her face. "Gotcha, loser." She cracked up.

JULY

Justine Anabeth Duchane lay on her boyfriend's chest on the hood of his green Jeep Cherokee, leaning against the windshield. It was a beautiful day. "So I finished another *Xanth* novel last night."

"You really do have a geeky side." They laughed.

"Well at least I don't have pimples or granny glasses," the politician quipped. They watched the summer breeze in the trees.

"Do you watch that British show about the dude in a police box," that made Matt's girlfriend laugh. He was jock. He liked swords and explosions.

"When it was on, it's no longer on PBS." She was a fan, yes. "Still a Trekkie."

"Oh no, we can't date anymore." Duchane looked up at her boyfriend and he cracked up. "Gotcha," she replaced her head, laughing. "But really? Star Trek?"

"Shut up." They laughed.

It was a good day.

"Hungry?" The question broke the perfect moment but not the perfect day.

"Yeah." They got off the Jeep and went to back. He opened the hatchback.

"You want to spread the blanket?" He had brought a blue blanket for the picnic.

Justine looked at him oddly. "Do you know me at all?" At that Matt just grinned.

She spread it out and he produced a couple beers, grapes in a Ziploc, crackers, cheese and some turkey sandwiches. That Saturday afternoon the world seemed to be on pause. It was nice. They opened the beer. "To three months."

She touched her lily necklace. She wore jeans and a cream t shirt with sneakers. He wore jeans and black CFD t shirt. "Too many more."

He pulled a box from the picnic basket. "For you."

"What?" She opened it. "Matt!" It was a birthstone charm, a 'J.'

"For the same gold necklace." She sat cross legged looking at him.

"You spoil me!" He shrugged and sipped his beer. She put it on her lap and undid the chain for the first time in a month, just long enough to add the J and then she replaced. "There."

"I claim you." He went to kiss her.

"*Claim* me cowboy?" She hesitated.

"With love." Now Justine kissed her man back.

"I love you too." That was a big step and they sat upright looking at each other silently. Then she picked up a sandwich. "What? Nobody ever fall in love with you before?"

"Uh...no actually. You're the first." She smiled.

"Hopefully I'll be the last," the politician didn't mean to say it. It also made her uncomfortable. But he never saw that. All the EMT saw was that beautiful smile.

No makeup. No effort. Hair in a ponytail, though shoulder length and curly, she made no effort to be beautiful. She didn't have to. Some things are self-evident. She was the most beautiful sight Mathew Jason Benson had ever seen. He lost himself in those eyes.

"Well isn't this joy?"

"One moment of perfect joy." They kissed again.

"Hey, you got that girls night out thing planned well?" He asked.

"Oh, Kelli and a few others, doing girly stuff," she furrowed her brow. "It's her birthday. Rather be with one of my boys." Her boyfriend or her best friend. *My boys--I like that.* That made Duchane smile. She took a bite.

"Your boys will be shooting pool tonight." The one game Matt had a chance beating Hal at. Hey, the writer was smart and a surprisingly good bowler.

"I'm so glad your guys are friends." Benson chuckled.

"Hal's great. Fun to hang with in groups or to go do guy stuff, I like him." Urban was from the Mark Twain school *it's better to remain silent and appear to be a fool rather than remove all doubt.* Hence the smaller man never pissed off bigger men.

"He likes you and his approval is important to me," every night, every single night for three months Hal had been Justine's last phone call. He was her voice of reason. Her best friend. "If he'd have disliked you, man I'd have kicked you to the curb."

"I don't blame you," Matt ate a grape. "Hard to have a friend like that." He at another.

"You and me," They just smiled. "This is real."

"Yes ma'am." They sipped their beer and enjoyed the beautiful summer day. Young love and a wonderful day. This was the best she could remember feeling.

This was the most real any relationship had every felt for him.

VII

You know the problem with perfect moments?

They end.

Justine Anabeth Duchane sipped her glass of wine and read from a Vic Victory novel:

Chapter One

"You can't pull that trigger," Ned Fitzgerald's seventy--year old eyes looked down the barrel unafraid

No it wasn't high art. It was a guilty pleasure.

It was welcome afternoon of quiet. One of her boys was at home preparing for an interview for staging his play and the other was working. "I love them both in different ways."

Another sip of wine. "Is that wrong?" Yes, Justine was asking herself. She looked up from the book. Duchane even answered herself.

"Of course not." The pillows were propped up on the bed. No, she never spilled the wine.

Then the other shoe fell.

The phone rang.

"Hello?" Well, who could it be?

"Justine." It was her father. Something was wrong. She sat up and dropped the novel

"Daddy?"

Justine loved her parents but she'd barely seen them since they moved to Chicago.

She was attached to her hometown.

"Hey Teeny," he had called her that since the first time he had held her in his arms. It embarrassed the politician all through her teens and now it made her feel all warm and fuzzy inside.

"Something's wrong." She tossed the blanket off her sweatpants.

"Your mom had a heart attack, she's lying in a hospital bed at Chicago Memorial," that took a moment to sink in. "Justine?"

"Sorry, dad." The younger Duchane swung her feet off the bed. "Did you just say what I think just said?" She stood up.

"It's bad. I don't think she has twenty-four hours left. She's still out." *Oh My God. Damn. Damn. Damn!*

"Dad, I'll be there tomorrow, I don't know how," did I mention that the politician was deathly afraid of planes, "but I'll be there before the end." That was a big promise.

"I love you Just,"--the elder Duchane's voice cracked. "Papa love Teeny."

"Too papa." She heard him trying to force a grin.

"See you soon." Click.

Quickly and without thinking Justine Anabeth Duchane dialed the first number that came to her head. "Hello," a voice spoke, looking up from his play.

"Hal." He could hear it. Something was wrong.

"What happened?"

"My mom had a heart attack, she's dying." He waited. "Oh man. I haven't seen her since Thanksgiving, we barely talk."

"Did you tell her you love her Justine?" The writer asked.

"What?" Justine was confused.

"Last time you spoke; did you say that?" The politician thought back.

"Yes." She was dumbfounded, pacing her little bedroom and holding her wine.

"Then that's what she will remember," her friend lied. But it's the words she needed to hear. Mom would remember thirty years not the last conversation, but this was a comfort and he knew it.

"Thank you." She finished the wine.

"Do you need anything? What can I do?" He was ready to jump.

"Ace your interview. Think of me. Answer when I call later." She thought for a minute. "I know you don't pray Hal."

"No, but I'll be thinking of you." She smiled. He was a good friend. "I'll be waiting by the phone." That was all a friend could be expected to do.

"Thank you. I'll talk to you later. I have to call Matt." It was seven PM. Hal's interview was first thing in the morning.

"Good luck." She hung up and dialed the firehouse.

"Cannonville firehouse." Justine didn't know the voice.

"Matt Benson please." She crossed her fingers that he wasn't out.

"Just a sec." Tick tock.

"Hello?" He seemed surprised.

"Matt. My mom had a heart attack, she's dying." That hit him fast.

"Justine? Let me just tell Jeremy. Hold on…. Hey Jeremy,"--she heard him talking. "How much sick time I got?" The question was muted.

"Oh I don't know," came a muffled voice in the distance. "Six or eight years."

"I'm leaving, personal emergency, be a couple days." He came back to the phone. "I'll be there in five, start packing, we'll get to Chicago as fast as the plane,"--

"Matt!" Justine interrupted. He hadn't given her a chance to talk. He was just fixing.

"I'm sorry. Are you okay? What?" He was not flunking, just at a loss and they were both flustered. He waited.

"I don't fly, I'm too scared." The big EMT didn't laugh.

"Then I'll drive you." Justine was too shocked to argue.

"I have to take a shower." She smelled of wine and felt dirty.

"I'll be there fast." Matthew Jason Benson hung up and ran to the stairs with Pamela Suzzette Tyler hot on his heels.

"Matt!" She called after him

"I'm late Pam," he ran through the back door.

"What is it!" She chased him. She was his partner after all.

"Justine's mom had a heart attack. I have to take her to Chicago." He opened the Jeep.

"Drive carefully," but he peeled out and did seventy on River Street. There was flashing lights in his window before he could blink.

"Fuck!" He pulled over in front of the boat house.

Out came two cops, a man on the passenger side and a woman on the left. She had a flashlight. When she recognized him, Captain Sarah Sullivan Hastings put the light down. "Where's the fire Benson?" She waived her patrolman off.

"Justine's mom had a heart attack, she needs me," the big EMT's desperation hung in Sully's ears. She nodded.

"Back in the car Porter." Then to Matt. "Give me the address and follow us. Police escort for a good EMT in a bad situation." He gave the cop the address and they pulled in front him.

No ticket but a knot in his stomach. They parted company at the townhomes. "Thank you, ma'am."

"Just drive carefully Matt," she looked maternally at him. Only about nine years separated them.

"You bet," he ran to the door. It was unlocked. Benson locked it behind him. He found his beloved sitting on the bed in clean black slacks and black sweater crying. "Justine."

"Hold me." He stood over her and held her close. Her tears stained his uniform and he didn't notice. Matt just waited for her to cry it out.

"I'm here. I can have you in Chicago by seven thirty Central, no problem." She looked up at him. Her eyes, tear filled, were full of disbelief.

"You what!" For a smart girl she can be dumb. To be fair, this ranked as one of the two worst days of her life after all.

"Throw on your bra, shoes and socks, pack a bag. I have my gym bag in the Jeep. I'll drive all night." He was in uniform already. That'd do. The EMT kissed the politician's forehead.

"You'd do that for me?" Justine couldn't believe how wonderful her boyfriend was.

"It's what I had in mind when I gave you this," he ran a finger along her necklace to the lily and the J.

"I love you," his girlfriend kissed him hard on the mouth.

"I love you too." She stood and went to tissues on the night table, wiping her eyes.

"There's a suitcase in the closet," She obeyed as Justine went to the dresser and got a bra and in that way men don't understand she put it on under the sweater, snapping it, never revealing anything.

"Okay," he spread the little blue suitcase, open, on the bed.

"Get the black formal dress, fold it in half and put it in," while the EMT did that his girlfriend got a few undergarments to zip into the top. "Two long sleeve shirts and two sweaters." Again, as her boyfriend obeyed the politician gathered socks and a pair of pantyhose that Benson had never had seen. "Three jeans and," but she was getting them herself, "three ts." Then she tapped her lips. "Brush and deodorant from the bathroom. Black shoes in the closet." He obeyed and Justine topped off with two pajama bottoms. He was amazed that she made it all fit neatly when closed up.

"Wow." She ignored him and pulled her socks on.

"Sneakers." Matt went back to the closet and watched his girlfriend put them on. "I'm forgetting something. He picked up the bag. "Kleenex," she grabbed the box by the bed. "There's bottled water in the fridge." Without a word the big EMT started walking. "Matt, I,"--Justine Anabeth Duchane put her arm around him. "Thank you."

"I believe that's in the duties of a boyfriend." She grabbed the waters and her keys off the counter, shutting lights off as she went.

"Let's go." After the door was locked they walked to his Jeep Cherokee. He opened her door and then put the suitcase in the hatchback.

"Your chariot is ready," he peeled out.

"I know you see death every day, but...hell...all four of my grandparents are still alive," so were three of his. "Death is new for me and I feel like a child afraid of the dark." The waters were in the console and she dipped into the tissues.

"But you're not alone," the Big EMT took his girlfriend's hand. "Never alone." Driving one handed Matt merged onto I-95 south.

"So much for believing in life after death," oh sure, she muddled the Nicene Creed on Christmas and Easter, but professing it halfheartedly and expecting it for your mom are too different things. "Some Catholic." Benson ran his hand up to her shoulder and rubbed.

"Angel, I won't tell you what to believe, but facing mortality the first time is always hard." He was right.

"What, are you a saint now?" That made him chuckle.

"It's not about seeing her in the hereafter. It's about missing the hell out of her in the meantime," the medical professional explained poetically. "Did I ever tell you how old I was when my grandpa died?" They were doing seventy in the left lane.

"No," Duchane looked at him with a bit of a vacant stare.

"I was sitting on his lap, five years old and he had just read me a story and kissed my head," Matthew Jason Benson explained, "that's the moment my mom's daddy died."

"That's horrible," the politician looked aghast and squeezed his hand.

"It was, at first. Even a bit scary. But I remember his funeral so clearly, Father Spellman, was preaching, and he said 'you will see Lee Homberg again. This is not end,' he quoted Churchill, 'this is not the beginning of the end, this is simply the end of the beginning.' Or, look at it this way. He is in a better position to love you; he is now your very own saint in Heaven praying for

you. He is still with you and you will see him again.'
That stuck with me and I never feared death again."

"That's incredible." She was moved. They drove in silence until the New York line. They let Webe 108 play and they held hands.

"We should stop for coffee, gas and bathrooms in Jersey since there are no rest areas in Pennsylvania," Matthew James Benson explained. "I've driven this way before. I can do it in one shot, don't worry."

"Don't you want to do it in shifts?" Duchane was perplexed.

"Nope, I'm used to doing all-nighters and double shifts in this job," with an ill-timed smirk he tapped his uniform and quickly put his hand back on the wheel. "You sleep, I'll drive."

"That's what I forgot. A pillow." She sighed.

"Do you want to go back?" Matt really didn't know what to say.

"No," the politician just studied his face. "Of course not."

"Okay." He wove through traffic; a bad habit you pick up driving an ambulance.

"My sister was always the strong one. My brothers are probably flaking out." She stared at the headlights. "Kathryn will be flying."

"Is she, how is she with airplanes?" Justine looked at him. "Sorry, stupid question."

"She'll take the red eye from LA." The big EMT tried to think. That's right. The sister worked at UCLA in the cafeteria. Long story, different book.

"What about Bobby and Lewis?" That was a whole other story.

"Well, Lewis works for dad and Bobby is a welder in the area so they'd be there already." They were.

He knew that. Matt felt foolish. "I'll get you there." There was, however, a sound coming from the passenger seat. It was not a pretty sound. Duchane was snoring, she had literally cried herself to sleep. Benson let go of her hand and patted it.

Later…

He parked at the last service area in Jersey and leaned over and kissed his girlfriend. She opened her eyes and kissed her boyfriend back. "Jersey?" She asked.

"Yeah." They got out of the car. "Do you want food?" He asked.

"Oh," Justine made a face. "I couldn't eat." He nodded. "Water."

"Of course." He headed to the McDonald's for coffee and probably water from tap," ah 1988 no bottled water in the vending machines and the shops were closed.

Duchane went to the payphone. "Justine?" Hal's voice came.

"Yeah, we're in Jersey, boy you should be sleeping." But she could hear him shaking his head. In fact, she usually knew what her friend was thinking.

"What are friends for? I should be with you," the writer knew he was wrong the moment he said it. "No, that's the realm of the boyfriend."

"I can't lose her." There was no sound until he spoke.

"I know but just remember something." She waited. "Your mom loves you wherever she is and you can love her wherever she is."

"Thanks Hal. You get some sleep." She hung up and went to the restroom. Though she knew they were pressed for time, she had to make a time consuming visit. The politician found the EMT waiting for her. The service area was all but deserted and needed cleaning.

"Ready?" she just nodded and took the paper cup of water. He had two large coffees in one big hand. "Need anything else?"

"No." She kissed him. "Sure you have enough coffee?" He split them between hands and held the door for her.

"No." She grinned. It was welcome sight. Outside on the roof of the Jeep was a pillow, in a clean silk pillowcase.

"What's that?" Matt looked at Justine and grinned.

"I bought it off a couple driving through. I explained why you needed it and they tossed in a clean pillowcase." He had overpaid.

"Wow." She kissed him again. "Thank you."

"You said you've driven this before?" He sighed as they got in. This story had not been told and he was embarrassed that he hadn't.

"When I was eighteen, that summer between high school and college--before I was an EMT," he drove to the gas pumps, "my football buddy Zak Isaacson and I wanted to see the country. We did Rose through South Dakota to LAX, then down to Monument Valley through Texas to Florida and then back north to home without seeing a hotel."

That made the politician smile. "That's the photo of you and the blonde guy in your apartment, at the Grand Canyon." He opened the window and waved to the attendant, fishing for his wallet.

"Yes it is. We took our time," he handed the man, tired in a Mobil uniform with gray hair who was about fifty, his credit card, "fill her with super." Matt popped the hood. "We saw everything we could. My eyes saw the Empire State Building, the steel mills of Pittsburgh, the desolation of Detroit and Chicago. We dipped a finger in Lake Superior. We walked the sands of Rooster Texas, the Vegas strip and of course we stood in awe at the Grand Canyon. I saw rich and poor; the hard working and the indigent."

And yet you're still a democrat. "You've mentioned those places before, but never really all at once. I didn't realize it was one trip."

"You're down a quart," the attendant showed Matt the dipstick.

"Top her off please." The man did just that. Full Service should really come back.

"It never came up before." He leaned back and sipped some coffee. "You know I never see Zak anymore. We talk a few times a year. I call him on Yom Kippur and he calls me on 'Zombie Jesus Day' and there's birthdays."

"Zombie Jesus Day?" He put the coffee in the console and fished for a five.

"Well He came back from the dead and that's pretty good for a Jewish friend." Matt chuckled. "Good old Zak." The attendant held the knucklebuster and the EMT signed. "Thanks." He gave the man a five and the man gave him his receipt.

"Thank you." They drove on.

There was construction. "Damn. I'll make up the time."

"I promise that when I'm your governor, while I won't be able to eliminate road construction, I will do my best to make it manageable," she had ideas.

"That would a tough thing to do with one hand while balancing the budget with the other." That brought Duchane to a more believable chuckle. "Let's get you on town council in November."

"I have big ideas and an uphill climb," the politician readjusted on her pillow and kicked off her sneakers. "Hope you don't mind."

"Not at all, it will probably help you sleep. It's a long drive and you have a big day tomorrow." Her boyfriend was empathetic and concerned.

"And it won't be hard on you?" Justine asked. "Or are you going to sack out at the hotel tomorrow?" Matt just sipped his coffee.

"Not at all. I planned to live on coffee and stay at your side," Benson explained. Duchane kissed her finger and put it to his lips.

"You know you're pretty amazing, right?" The EMT grinned.

"I hear that a lot." He glanced at his girlfriend and after a pregnant pause and despite herself she burst out laughing with insane laughter. Boy did she need that. Sometimes you have to forget the pain to make it through the night.

"Nah," Matt was chuckling. "I have lots of flaws."

"You don't drink to excess. You don't sleep around. You respect women. You barely swear. You're sweet and romantic. Shit Matt, how many boyfriends of three months would drop everything and shatter his perfect attendance to do this for me?" She could have gone on but stopped when she saw her boyfriend was blushing.

"What did you say courage was in your column?"

"I feel like I'm in an old movie and you're Gary Cooper or Cary Grant." He raised an eyebrow.

"Cary Grant? James Stewart please." That made her giggle. He had succeeded in lightening the mood. He didn't think of himself as a matinee idol.

"What do you think are your flaws?" Justine was curious.

"I often say the wrong thing and I'm often dense." He shrugged. "I dunno, you put me on the spot here angel." They were almost through the traffic.

"It's endearing." He sighed.

"Hey, want to hear a joke?" Why not try?

"No, okay. Sure." Why not? It'd take her mind off it.

"Man walks in a bar. He says ow." There was silence for a moment and then finally Duchane laughed. Benson shrugged.

"Lame." She blew her nose.

"A priest, a minister and a rabbi walk into a bar and the bartender say there must be a joke in here somewhere." Not even a chuckle. "Bad timing?"

"Bad joke." She squeezed his leg.

"Tough audience." She giggled.

"It's not a good night." She got comfortable. "Is my hair pretty Matt?"

"Of course," but she was snoring already.

VIII

Justine was sleeping in the passenger seat and she looked angelic; even with her head back and her mouth open. Matt would never bring himself to tell her that she was a snorer. In Indiana he had to pee like race horse and gas was low. He parked and got out quietly, leaving her sleeping. He then tossed his empty coffee cups in the nearest trash and went inside. He reappeared with two more coffees and got back in the car.

At the pump he planned it better and handed the young blonde attendant a five and his credit card. The oil was topped off again. "Where are we?" Duchane mumbled, sitting up.

"Indiana." Justine stretched. He accepted the card and receipt and drove around.

"I left you that long?" The big EMT just shook his head. He had heard plenty of pop music to go with her snoring. Justine pulled her sneakers on.

"You were here." He pulled back around and parked. "Need to pee?"

"Yeah, thanks." She got out, still stretching.

"Want something to eat or drink?" Matt called out the window.

"Nah, I don't feel like coffee." She called back. After she peed she dialed Chicago Memorial with her father's calling card. Ah the eighties.

"Good morning,"--the switchboard operator was too chipper.

"Laura Duchane's room please." There was a buzz.

Her father answered, he was not sleeping. "Yes."

"Daddy, it's me." She heard him perk up.

"Teeny." There was murmuring on her end. "Where are you?"

"Indiana, Matt's been driving." He didn't respond. "We're making great time."

"Mom hasn't woken up. I got you a room at the Sheraton nearby. Should I--naw, you're thirty you two can share a room." *How progressive dad.* "Papa love Teeny."

"Too papa. Thank you. I'll be there, I promise." There was another pause.

"I know." She hung up and returned to her boyfriend.

"Let's go." She buckled up. It was still dark

"At your service ma'am." She sipped her water and he sped in the left lane.

"Matt, *my* knees are sore. Yours must be in agony." He shook his head.

"I'm used to it and I'll take a hot shower later. There's Tylenol in the glove compartment if you need it, aspirin would be better, sitting this long can cause blood clots. That's in there too." Smirking, his girlfriend opened the door and got the aspirin.

"You think of everything don't you?" He sighed.

"I'll get you there, that's all that matters." Duchane took too pills and replaced the bottle.

"You should have been a chauffeur; you'd have made a killing." That made the big EMT laugh.

"Nah, I like talking to my customers too much." That was true. He was a talkative one in the ambulance, drove Pam crazy.

"My dad booked me a room at the Sheraton, he said I'm old enough to have you sleep over." They looked at each other for a moment and shrugged. Not the time.

"Is it near the hospital? Because I don't want you walking around that city without a bodyguard," which Benson assumed would be him.

"Oh, you are getting the best backrub, first chance we get." That sounded promising.

Matthew Jason Benson took Justine Anabeth Duchane's hand and they crossed into Illinois.

"Welcome to the land of Lincoln."

"Birthplace of Ronald Reagan that has dissolved into a cesspool of liberalism." The democrat driving let her have that one. She was hurting. "Mark my words Matt, the first communist president will come from Chicago."

"If you say so," truth was he didn't understand half of what she said when she talked politics. Half of what he understood he disagreed with, but he kept his mouth shut.

Justine didn't talk much more during the straight shot to Chicago. They even missed rush hour traffic and as promised Benson parked in the hospital visitor's lot fifteen minutes before seven. Forty-five minutes early.

"Did I doze off again?" Duchane stretched. The driver shook his head. She had been mostly quiet, which told him she had been awake.

"Not long." Then they got out of the car and locked the front doors. She watched her boyfriend open the hatch back.

"Are you staying in uniform?" She asked.

"Yeah, in uniform I can walk around any hospital like I own the place." That was true. The politician smoothed his shoulders.

"I want you to look good for my family." She took out her ponytail. "Mom doesn't like my hair back." That was a point of contention with Duchane women.

Matt stretched his legs as his girlfriend opened the suitcase, got her brush and made her hair fall around her face. She liked it. "You look amazing."

She tossed the brush in. "Whatever." He locked up and they went in the main entrance of the sprawling monstrosity of a hospital. Everything in Chicago is *big*.

An elderly woman stood up. She was dressed in a brown Nancy Reagan ensemble. Her hair was even the same style. "I'm sorry, it's not visiting hours."

"Laura Duchane's room." Benson stood to his full height and came close in the woman's face. "She's family," the lady sat and flipped pages. "Quite quickly, please."

She wrote in down. "I'm sorry," Justine accepted it.

"Thank you," it was barely a whisper and, despite never having been there before, the big EMT navigated the confusing hallways and elevators to the ICU.

"Are you ready?" He asked as they approached the door.

"Of course not," he put his arm around her and knocked on the door. It opened slowly. Robert Duchane Sr. was a short and powerfully built man in his sixties with iron gray hair and little body fat. A bit more James Garner than Don Johnson.

"Teeny," she separated from her boyfriend and hugged her father. "You must be Matt," the older man spoke when he'd released his daughter.

"Yes." The younger man tried not to stammer and they shook.

"Come in, meet Bobby," Robert Junior had gotten his father's name--all of it. Love trumps blood but he looked like the woman in the bed, chestnut hair and cheekbones right down to the nose. He was dressed in jeans and a Bulls jersey. "Lewis," if his dad looked like old James Garner, Lewis looked like young James Garner, complete with cowboy boots, Wrangler jeans and western style dress shirt then there was Kathryn. She was her sister but plumper. She wore a blue dress down to her ankles. The newcomer shook everyone's hands.

His girlfriend ran to her mother's bedside and knelt. "Mommy. Don't go," she sounded girlish, not like an educated woman of thirty.

The woman in the bed was beautiful, like her daughter. The elder had a small breathing mask on and the hospital blanket covered the gown. There were beeping machines and the EMT knew what they all meant. It wasn't good.

"How is she?" He asked Robert.

"The doctor said any minute two hours ago." Justine stood up and began to shift her weight back and forth. Benson went to chart at the foot of the bed and opened it. Then he closed his eyes. *Damn.* "Can you read those Matt?"

"Well enough." The door opened and a handsome young priest came in with four coffees.

"Oh no, I'm short." He frowned. "Sorry."

"This is Father Cal from Holy Name Cathedral, he anointed her already and is keeping watch with us." He took the coffees, one stack on another in two hands from the young clergyman. "This is Justine's young man."

"You must be Matthew." They shook.

"Nice to meet you father and I don't need any more coffee." He looked at his girlfriend who came to his side and the EMT put his arm around her.

"I'm good Padre." She shook his hand too.

"Just-ine," the figure in the bed had pushed the oxygen mask aside and spoke. They all looked at her and her elder daughter ran to her side, taking her hand. Then she told her daughter something she had not said since high school. "Your hair looks beautiful." Laura Duchane smiled and then breathed no more.

The Machine beeped louder. The other siblings crowded together. Benson flipped the machine off and put his arm around his beloved. It was over.

Justine had made it.

They had made it.

"You have my condolences," Father Cal crossed himself and then blessed the family, couldn't hurt right.

A nurse came in and looked at Matt. "You on duty?" She was red haired and fifty wearing beige scrubs.

"He's family," Bobby explained.

Wordlessly the nurse pulled the blanket over the deceased and double checked the machines. "I'll leave you to your goodbyes."

"We need to meet father, plan the funeral," Robert whispered, holding back the tears.

"There will be time for that,"--but the older man cut him off.

"I want the funeral day after tomorrow, everyone is in town or near enough." The presbyter nodded. "Can I see you tomorrow to plan?"

"Two PM alright?" The widower nodded. "Do you want me to call the funeral home…"

"Please," and Father Cal left.

"Where's Grandpa James and Grandma Laura," Justine's mom's parents.

"One their way from Maine, they'll be here today," Kathryn sighed. "I have to call Grandpa Sam," Duchane, "he's starting a phone tree." She left the room, wanting to be away from the body, Lewis followed her. Grandma Ella Duchane was in a hospice with dementia but was healthy.

"I want to stay with mom until they come get her," Justine explained.

"All right," her father told her. "Then we're going to IHOP."

It was probably good the aunts and uncles, cousins and grandparents weren't there. The room had been too crowded for the ICU as it was.

IX

"So what is it with Teeny?" Matt asked her papa over pancakes.

"Um," Justine blushed.

"Ever since she was an infant," Robert put his arm around his elder daughter. "It's a play on T-I-N-E, as in,"--

"Justine," he caught up.

"This," he put his arm around Kathryn Alexandrina Duchane, "is Drina, from her middle name." Kathryn buried her face in her hands and blushed.

"He just called me Junior," Bobby explained. Love trumps blood, every time.

"That's *who* you are; Robert Lewis Duchane Junior," yeah, he was all Duchane.

"And Lewis?" Matt asked.

"I'm Lad. Lewis Alfred Duchane." he chuckled. "Could be worse.

"Mom was the formal one," Justine explained.

"Oh man," her father put his hands on the table and looked down. "What am I gonna do without her?"

"Daddy, you're sixty-three. You are a beacon of health," Kathryn explain. "You got nothing but time. Look at Uncle Charlie, He's seventy and with all his problems he looks fifty."

Justine spoke up. "You'll go back to work next week, take one step after another,"--

"I don't want my job. I want my next twenty-five years with your mother," Robert whispered in agony. No one knew what to say. So they were silent.

"She was my mom, dad and I can move forward. I may not have been a mama's boy but we were close." Bobby spoke rubbed his hands together. "Her cholesterol was high and she had heart problems her whole adult life."

"Why didn't I hear any of this?" Justine asked.

"If I didn't live with them the last couple years, I may not have heard," Bobby went on.

"I didn't know either," Kathryn explained.

"That wasn't fair of her," Lewis chimed in.

Matt took it in. This was family. He liked it. Big families are beautiful.

"It's what she wanted," the patriarch finished the thought and silence reigned again.

"Remember when I cut my bangs in high school," the politician changed the subject. That turned her father's mood. "She hated that."

"Or when she decided to get the tattoo?" Bobby suggested. His sister's facepalmed.   "Tattoo?" Benson asked confused.

"Mom, not Justine," Lewis explained. "She was into unicorns and mermaids. She had a mermaid on her shoulder blade.

Robert smiled. "That was no Disney character." He sighed. "She wanted a Yankee insignia, I talked her out of it."

"Why?" Matt asked.

"Too masculine. But I'll honor her last request." He sipped some water sadly. "At least I get to be in New York for a day.

"What?" His children asked together.

"I'm scattering her ashes at Yankee Stadium so she will never have to miss another home game, it was he dying wish. She made me promise if she went first…" rubbing his eyes, Robert stopped talking.

"Cremation?" Younger daughter was in shock. "Mom needs a grave and place we can leave flowers." She was perturbed.

"You never visited her or sent flowers when she was alive," elder sister argued. "None of us did, we're all guilty."

"It's okay girls. She loved you and was proud." He put his arms around his daughters. "Cremation is what she wanted, that's what she's getting, *and I* am paying after all."

"What about Holy Name?" Lewis interrupted.

"Can we even do that without a body?" Kathryn asked, in a blonde moment.

"She'll be cremated after the funeral," Lewis explained.

"Oh." She was still appalled. The rest of the family started eating again so the EMT did as well.

"Three-hour viewing tomorrow?" Bobby asked.

"I have to meet with the funeral home director, but I assume it will be six to nine," the patriarch explained. "Damn. I don't want to go through this week."

"We have to go shopping today," Kathryn told her father. "You need a suit."

"Drina, I haven't worn a suit in forty years, it's not my thing. I built this company with your uncle and my sleeves rolled up." He wore Khakis and button downs, sometimes sweaters. That was it. Charlie was more formal.

"Dad!"

"You go shopping," he fished for his wallet. "Take my credit card, you know what would look good." His daughters sighed.

"Dad," they facepalmed. "You need to be measured." But he just shook his head and ate some bacon. It was quiet for moment.

"Where are you going?" Benson took that moment to ask his girlfriend's sister.

"Oh, a place in the mall. Bobby uses it and it's good for formal wear." She looked at Justine. "You want to come?"

"I have to bring Matt anyway, he won't let me walk this city alone, he's afraid of crime," her father grinned.

"Good boy." He then guzzled coffee.

"He also needs a suit." The EMT shrugged.

"As long as I'm not a third wheel." The Duchane sisters shook their heads.

"It's a plan," their father said.

"So how long have you two been together?" Lewis asked, pushing his plate away.

"Three months," his sister explained.

"That's a good boyfriend," Bobby argued. "Keep him."

X

After an interminable funeral and endless funeral brunch, pain and depression and no one wants to eat at those things Justine and Matt said goodbye to the immediate family and twenty or so others he had met and then, at her father's insistence they were back in the car. Dad had booked a hotel on the Western Ohio border and told them to take their time driving home, but wanted to make sure they didn't miss any more work than they had to.

`   They changed into jeans and t shirts for the ride. No thank you to formal wear. This time Duchane was awake for the ride. "Poor Hal did that whole mailer by himself."

"He's good campaign manager and good friend," again the big EMT found himself praising Urban. Hey, his closest friend was a sassy twenty-three-year-old girl.

"Yes he is." Justine kicked her shoes off. It was about one.

"Are you...I mean how are you feeling today?" The boyfriend asked.

"Thank God it's over, that's all I can say." She leaned back.

He reached over and squeezed her leg through her jeans. They were probably fine legs. She liked it and it was new thing in their relationship. "You did well." He took his hand away.

"So did you." She sighed. "Remember how dad proposed to her?" Benson looked blank and stared ahead, doing seventy in the left lane.

"Erm,"--he couldn't remember.

"I told you that story," still he looked blank so his girlfriend went on. "The box, the note, how is…" Still nothing.

"Shit, I'm sorry." She looked ahead.

"Oh well." It was one mistake in a week of awesomeness. "You were a trooper."

And he was for many hundred miles until their Sheraton.

They talked of many things.

They sat in silence.

They argued music.

They played the Trivial Pursuit cards her father had insisted they take.

They didn't fight.

"My family likes you, dad says you are a real hero." Matt didn't feel like one.

"It was my duty and my honor," her boyfriend was starting to sound like a broken record.

"I feel like I owe you a reward," she had said that not too long ago in very different circumstances. Little did she know that one would turn out more exciting.

The driver didn't want anything. "When I lose someone you can come with me." Duchane looked at Benson, dejected.

"I'm buying you a steak dinner tonight." That was a good thing. He liked that plan.

"That works for me," they grinned.

After checking in they found a steakhouse, it was rocking and full of people of all ages. Their waitress were cowgirl boots, a tight mini skirt, a low cut pink top and had a pout under her black silky hair. I tell you this because Benson didn't notice, which made her pout more.

"Fill up my white wine and if it gets low bring me another," the waitress knew what Duchane meant. It was time to mourn the old fashioned way.

"One beer." Matt was too busy drinking in his girlfriend's eyes.

"I'll be right back." The waitress shook her ass away. Still, the big EMT did not notice.

"Do you know what you want?" He asked his Justine.

"To hold you all night." That sounded good. They had shared a room the two nights in Chicago but there was little touching and precious little sleeping. "And to give you that back rub."

The politician finished her wine. The waitress brought the bottle and found the couple holding hands. "Do you know what you want?" She asked.

"Two of the most expensive steaks you serve with baked potatoes and house dressing on the salads. He wants his well done and I want mine rare." Cowgirl boots didn't even try to get the menus.

Duchane had another glass and another. "Are you sure you don't want to slow down?"

"No," She explained. "Not tonight. Tonight I drink."

"All right." She wasn't driving. "I love you and I don't care if it's one day, one year, thirty years or fifty years I love you Justine Anabeth Duchane."

"Well, Matthew Jason Benson, I love you more." She giggled. "After dinner I was thinking of a more enjoyable reward."

"Um, flattering, but let's table that for now." He scrambled for topic to change the subject. "Do you want to see anything tomorrow or do you want to drive straight through."

"Jeremy is expecting you. We drive." She grinned.

"Okay. What about Lenor at Oberon?" She had been secretive on her schedule.

"She gave me the rest of the week for bereavement with pay, she said Tuesday. Which is good I need to get a handle on the campaign by Monday." She belched and covered her mouth blushing. "Excuse me." It was actually cute.

"There is no excuse." They laughed.

The country radio in that cowboy restaurant seemed to be attuned to their mood.

They got the giggles before they got their steaks. Outside the window it began to rain and they had walked from the hotel.

When Matt saw that he knew it was clique and he knew what was going to happen and he knew he wanted it to. She had a plan to reward him. It wasn't what he had planned but desire had taken hold of him and she was ready.

XI

Hal stayed up half the night. He got the mailing done. Then he highlighted phone lists. Then he worked on another play. *Hey, Woody Allen writes every damn day.* He was basing a love story on how Robert Duchane had asked Laura Duchane to marry him. He kept looking at the clock. Tick tock. Last call?

The storm moved east. The clock ticket.

The hour of the wolf chimed.

The phone hadn't rung.

The writer wrote.

He screamed to the God he wasn't sure existed to protect his friend.

The writer wrote.

He would never have finished *Nine Innings* without Justine.

He would never have finished two more.

The phone rang. "Justine?"

"Hal?" She was ebullient.

"Yes." She was okay. He was relieved.

"Matt and I made love tonight. I feel wonderful." Why didn't he?

"That's great. I'm glad you're happy." Benson wasn't the type to take advantage of a vulnerable woman...but something didn't sit right. It was their first time together.

"Thank you. He's coming out of the bathroom. Did you hear from Cannonville Playhouse?" She asked. He smiled faintly.

"October twenty-first until November third," or the week before Election Day. "*Nine Innings* plays in Cannonville and opening night I get a check for ten thousand."

"That's awesome." There was murmuring. "Good night bud."

"Night." Click

XII

Hal wrote a sonnet.

Love is not always your friend

And it is often disguised

Love can be your enemy

Not knowing your feelings

Not knowing your heart

Are mistakes

Find out who you are.

Find out what you want.

.   Then he called the one uncle he got along with. "Hello?"

"Rusty? I uncle Dave there?" The teenager laughed. Russell James Blaudel was almost ready for college, practically engaged to his high school sweetheart and a far wiser man than his cousin Hal.

"No, he and mom went to dinner, what's up Horatio." His family always insisted on calling the writer that—that's why they talked so little. Even though the Blaudels were close a different religion than Urban, Dave's wife was Hal's mom's older sister and they were really close.

"I needed advice. It's not important." There was murmuring in the background. That had to be Kitty—Kathleen Slater, Rusty's girlfriend.

"I'm here if you need something Horatio," There was a long pause. "Hal?"

"It's, it's romance stuff. Don't worry about it bud." How could he talk about this with a kid a decade younger than himself.

"Whatever it is Horatio, if you talk to her, it will be better than if you don't," like I said. Far wiser than his cousin Hal.

"You're right Rusty. Thanks." The younger cousin hung up the phone.

"Who was that?" Kathleen Slater asked. She was a sporty teen with a pixie cut. She always wore sneakers and if she could, shorts.

"My cousin Hal." Russ shrugged. "He's got girl trouble."

Kitty kissed her young man. "Aren't you glad you don't have those problems?"

"I talk to you. That's the secret. No secrets, right?" She nodded with a grin.

PART THREE
"A politician cares about the next election; A Statesman about the next generation."

--Joe Arcudi, First Selectman, Westport CT 1993-1997

Fall From Grace

1988

The Play

I

Theodore Roosevelt Maguire looked at the two newspapers on his desk. OBERON COMMUNITY NEWSPAPERS ENDORSES THESE CANDIDATES FOR TOWN COUNCIL TOM ARMBRUSTER JUSTINE DUCHANE AND FLORA JONES. The other was a different type of advertisement. OBERON COMMUNITY NEWSPAPERS PRESENTS THE TENTH ANNUALLY OPEN WRITERS WINNER AT THE CANNONVILLE PLAYHOUSE: NINE INNINGS OF LIFE BY HAL URBAN.

Lenor entered the office with glass of water. "Did you take your pill Theodore?" He rubbed his side where his second kidney used to be. He felt...happy.

Maybe someday he could look Justine Ducane in the eye, as he now he looked Lenor in the eye. "Thank you." This was a good moment of change.

"Your welcome," she kissed his forehead.

"I'm ready to step down. Have you decided who will take over?" The big man asked.

"Pete Shafer is ideal to be a full time editor, if you want us to run the paper together; it will be in good hands." Maguire smiled.

"Good. Then I'm going to concentrate on the foundation." Lenor sat down across from him as proud as she could be if she was his mother. *You were right old friend.*

"Caught the bug, huh?" He was now a giver.

On the wall behind him was the last article he'd ever write. Before Bad Vlad, uncle Vlad had died, the editor had been a good newspaper writer. Truthfully, he missed the old bastard. He did love his uncle. He also loved his dad.

The article headline was: SERIAL ATTACKER PLEADS GUILTY: NO DAY IN COURT. Duchane would not have to testify.

"Do you want to come to dinner with me and dad?" Mac asked Lenor.

II

Pamela Suzzette Tyler brought a civilian in the weight room where her partner was lifting. She looked at the woman as if to say *you're welcome.* The younger one carried a Chinese food bag.

"Matt, this is my sister, Carolyn." Carolyn Tyler, 30, was short and plump with blonde hair. Benson thought she was beautiful. She was night and day from her sister. He felt guilty and thought of Justine.

"Hello Matt." She held out her hand. *Too bad he's taken. He'd be good for Carolyn,* the younger Tyler thought to herself. Pamela was never the woman for the big EMT. This isn't one of those stories.

He sat up. "Nice to meet you." They shook hands.

"She brought lunch for me, but you're my best friend man," that was the first time one of them admitted it.

"I'm glad to meet you Carolyn." Jeremy came in.

"Hey, who is this?" The bald man asked carrying an envelope.

"This is her sister, relax, they're going to eat." The Tylers left the room. Then the captain sat next to his protégé.

"Matt, I want to talk to you." Well, he was doing that.

"Am I dying?" The boss didn't blink. "Are you dying?" The older man didn't laugh.

"You've been spending too much time with Pamela." Benson just chuckled.

"Seriously, what's up?" This was not a joke.

"Ever think about a promotion?" Seriously? Now. What an honor.

"What's this?" He accepted the envelope.

"You have to go up to Hartfield for the test, but I think you should take it next week and get fast tracked for promotion. You could have my job in two years." The big man pulled the documents out.

"You already enrolled me?" He flipped through it.

"You're the best EMT I have, I won't waste that."

III

FRIDAY

The last day they worked together.

"So, this is your last day?" Bertram Bryan Booker rolled in after Horatio Albert Urban. No surprise, that was true every morning since The Friendship had taken his friend away. Every morning but one. The writer looked up from a Yankees article.

"Yup. Oberon Community Newspapers will need to make do without me after today." He smiled. Two weeks of on sight rehearsals and then he'd be trading his wares. Even if he was one and done he was finished at the paper. "They'll probably be better off."

"We probably will," Monica called from her office door in her low cut red dress.

"Thanks," Hal called back and went back to typing.

"Though the last six months your performance has improved," Men noticed her. Book noticed her. Hal ignored her. She had no power over him now.

"You were right all along," Book defended his friend. "He doesn't belong here."

"Probably so, but if your plays are as riddled with typos as your columns and articles your reign as the next Bill Shakespeare will be short." The writer stood up, picked up a legal sized envelope and walked around his desk.

He had grown some balls in the last six months. "When you know him as well as I do Monica, you can call him Bill." He slammed the envelope against her belly and she took it. "Until then, the name is Mister William Shakespeare."

"Whatever," Booker's boss turned and slammed her door.

"What's in the envelope?" Book asked and Hal returned to work

The Box, his third play he'd finished that year. Flawlessly edited. *Thank you Miss L.,* it was a surprise. "Another play." Urban went back to work.

"Not gonna miss her?" The heir to Billy Dee asked, sitting in his chair.

"Nah." They laughed.

"So you found a lady friend yet good buddy?" Book asked.

"Right here." Hal was joking and his friend didn't understand why he picked up a pen.

"Who?" The writer laughed.

"My art." Booker sighed.

"I always loved you brother, but you used to be a self-absorbed, conceited, ill-mannered, alcohol ridden, cowardly, unreliable prick." Book didn't pull punches.

"Thanks for sugar coating it." They laughed. "And now?"

"You don't drink. You pay attention to other people and their needs, Justine will be elected because of you. You are on time for work and you appear to have learned how to stand up for yourself. What happened in Massachusetts?" Had he come that far?

The offices were crowded. Men and women typed, shuffled papers and worked the phones.

Hal evaded the question. "An entity that doesn't grow is dying."

"You also got more poetic," his friend told him. "Much more than you used to be."

"Guess I'm closer to the source." He changed pages.

"Source?" Booker, in auburn silk suit and gray silk shirt, red tie leaned forward confused. Hal was in a new green sweater and jeans.

"The muses, the bards, the poets and the playwrights of old." He was on a roll and it made him smile. "The great novelists…"

"The Muses?" Book cracked up. "You've been touched by the strippers in Rose, haven't you?" Yes that was the name of a strip club.

"No," but it made Urban crack up. "I mean like the beings in Greek mythology that inspire writers and artists."

"Interesting, I didn't know strippers were so powerful." Loneliness had once brought the writer to the wrong muses and if it had to do with women, well, Booker knew it.

"They don't have that kind of power, if they did I'd have gotten rich a long time ago and Jimmy Swaggart would still be a minister." The two old friends laughed.

"And several politicians would still have jobs." That's why Booker wanted Justine to win. "Women don't do that shit," or so he thought. Little does he know. "And forget Monica, she can't touch you." A nod.

"Well the only team I care about is the Yankees and this season is over for them." He typed that out in proper English.

"That's your article. The decline and fall of the Yankees Empire?" Booker smiled at the play on Justine's column.

"Good title." The writer was learning that the universe had a sense of humor.

Justine Anabeth Duchane walked up to Horatio Albert Urban's desk. "Well, if Mohamed won't come to mountain. Good timing.

"You know," Monica was out of her office again, walking by, "for a guy serving out his notice you are here a bit early for my taste." She was annoyed that Urban was on time.

"You like the play Mon?" He sneered. Of course she hadn't read it.

"I can ask Lenor to give *you* the day off," Duchane called after Shafer who hoofed away.

"I bet you won't miss that bitch." Yes, 'that bitch's' husband was now the editor and Justine was staying--for now. Town council is a part time job.

"I meant to be over there when she came in." He jumped up. "An agent asked to represent me this morning." He stood face to face with her. "Permission to hug."

"Permission granted." The hugged deeply and it truly felt safe.

"I have an army," they separated. "Doctor Burma and her husband, also Doctor Burma, her sister Ellis, Book and Kelli Jones all ready to make calls for you."

"You have time for it with the play?" He grinned.

"That was the deal. Last mailing went out yesterday." That made Justine's day.

"Thank you, but... What about Coyt? What about the agent?" She asked. This was new for her since Massachusetts, she wanted everyone else's news.

"Max is a shithead but all of his staged plays are read by actors and agents and directors before they start production. I got lucky." Maybe he wouldn't hire that agent, maybe he would. "Coyt says I should be kissing his feet for the ten grand because I'm an unknown but I like the director and the technical director so it's okay.

"And the acting?" He grinned.

"My lead is a bit younger than expected, but my Lou dead ringer for the player I based the ghost on. All three leads really understand the story." He picked up another manila envelope.

"And here is a better play." She opened it and pulled the first page out.

"*The Box* dedicated to--my mom?" He grinned. Justine was moved.

"Your parents inspired it." The politician hugged her friend again.

"Thank you Hal, it's like you've made her immortal." He shrugged.

"It was selfish, it's good art." But Duchane furrowed her brow.

"It's something a friend would do Urban." He put his hands out, palms up and they laughed.

"You know I want to sit in on a rehearsal. You better make that happen." She gave her best friend the smolder.

"I can make that happen," he gestured. "Walk with me."

"Why? Does the sports room have ears?" Everywhere. "What do you want to know?"

The writer whispered when they were alone in the copy room, door closed. "Why do you call me from his bed?"

The politician blushed. He was her last phone call. "Do you figure that out?"

"Every time." He walked a step and turned away. "I listen to you. I pay attention. I know you. You're my best friend. I know when you say something and I know when you don't say something and I always know what you mean."

Duchane was a little confused. "Hal, I," she put the play down. "I want to share happy moments with my best friend and you *are* my last phone call *every* night." A hand took Urban's shoulder. He did not move.

"Wasn't he saving himself for marriage?" She giggled.

"Did you buy that one?" That was a good question.

"I don't know." The writer turned to the politician. "Some things I don't need to know."

"Are you judging me?" The hand dropped.

Hal laughed. "Me? Judge anyone?" It took Justine a moment but she laughed as well.

"Good." He sighed.

"Do you love him?" She bit her lip. No matter what she said he knew the real answer.

"Of course I love him." *I love the idea of him. He makes me happy. He's hot. We have good times. There's a spark.* Her manner, her face said everything but what her mouth said.

Her friend knew and he would not say a word. He'd let her live the life that made her happy because that's what friends do. "Good."

"Thank you." Duchane hugged him "You are my best friend."

"Thank you." He sat on some boxed of copy paper. "The technical director at the playhouse Emma is our age, red haired and cute. I asked her to coffee in the morning." He didn't want to, but if the writer was going to live he had to date.

The politician beamed. "That's great."

"She said no." They frowned. "She doesn't date co-workers. I figure she just thinks I'm ugly that's usually the case."

"You aren't ugly Hal," Justine lowered her voice. "I find you attractive."

"But I'm not Matt," take that how you want.

"That's not fair! That's a different kind of love." He knew that. She crossed her arms. "I don't want to imagine life with you in it and my campaign would be nothing without you."

"And these plays, the drinking--without you I'd be screwed. I know that. I'm so much better than I was in April." He stood up. "You deserve to be with a guy like Matt, handsome, thoughtful and romantic. A man of the same background." It sounded flat.

"You say that like you're checking things off." Duchane giggled.

"Who said I didn't?" Urban tried to smirk. "I had high standards for the man for you. I care too much about you not to."

"Wow," the politician was floored. "Thank you," she told him, taking a step back. "That's amazing. What a friend you are."

"Are we good?" Justine took his shoulder again.

"Better than good." They went to the door.

"So why are you doing everything right for the paper this last week?" He shrug

"Staying in practice."

IV

Cannonville News Arts and Leisure

By, Roberta Black

Last night the big auditorium at Cannonville Playhouse was standing room only for the first time all season. The underdog winner of the $10,000 prize for unsolicited manuscript Nine Innings of Life by Oberon Community Newspapers' own Hal Urban has not only won the prize but the hearts of every person in that building. In this theater critic's humble opinion, the play will easily be picked up for a twelve city in twelve-month tour of New England.

The poignant tale of a Jewish man who loves baseball and business who learns, perhaps too late, what it means to be a father reaches the most gripping heights of human drama. The play is a personal one, based on men in Urban's own family. On the final night the writer will presented

citations by First Selectman Hal Opus and Senator Ross Magee.

V

"I don't understand why their having another dress rehearsal mid-run?" Justine asked Thursday night. She sat on her bed in old sweats and a plain t shirt.

"Ordinarily they want to put their best foot forward on the second Friday because that's the day the prospective theater managers and producers from a possible run are in the audience." Hal sat on his couch, feet up, jeans and a Mets t shirt. There was some typing on hold. Yes, he was on a roll.

"Which mean tomorrow night decides the future of *Nine Innings*?" That made the politician smile. She sipped a Lipton iced tea can next to the bed.

"Yes." He didn't tell her two agents had asked for copies of *The Box*--that was a surprise, or the writer hoped. "Everyone in the building is rooting for me, except Coyt--it's like he wants me to fail.

"Well, he'd be a fool not to go through the motions to support you, did he see the review Roberta Black gave you? I mean come on." They shared a laugh. It *had* been glowing. The sellouts though, that was all Urban, people wanted to see the play.

"Yes, it is almost like someone is looking out for me." Hal reached for his hot chamomile, Mr. Karlson's drink of champion writers.

"Almost like a guardian angel?" That made Urban laugh. Duchane didn't.

"More like Lenor controlling the theater column and the ad space." Justine just sighed.

"Does that bother you?" She looked at her toes. The pink was chipped. They needed painting. Maybe midnight blue in honor of her friend's play about Yankee fans.

"What if a good chunk of money came from the paper?" As of yet she didn't know who owned Shumay LLC and contributed so much to her campaign all the politician knew was that the writer was going to get her elected.

"Do you think Lenor or Mac is capable of that much muscle in town?" There was a long pause and Urban realized that love and truth should go hand in hand. Another growth moment.

"Mac owns Shumway LLC. The huge contribution you received was all him. He wants you to get elected." There was a long pause.

"What? Why? How do you know this?" Duchane was mad and Hal hesitated.

"The day I got my stitches out I visited him in a hospital room. He told me what he was doing and asked for my promise not to tell you." There it was, Urban couldn't hide the truth.

"What, why would he do that?" Justine spilled her iced tea. "Damn." She got out of bed and picked it up. Then she went in the bathroom to get a towel and cleaner.

"Because he doesn't want anything from you, he just disappeared. He doesn't run the paper he's fallen off the map." That was true. The writer waited for the politician to speak.

"Ugh, sorry I spilled my Lipton. Why....why was he in the hospital?" OCD girl was kneeling down cleaning her carpet the way she wanted to clean up Cannonville government.

"I think he donated a kidney." They didn't speak for a minute.

"Theodore Roosevelt Maguire Junior donated a kidney?" Justine couldn't believe it. "That's not in his nature."

"Something was different about him. I tried to ask but he wouldn't tell me." Hal swung his legs down and took a long swig of his hot drink.

"Odd. Anyway, according to the polls I really think I have a chance to win." Leaning on the bed Justine stood up.

"What are friends for?" He stood and stretched. "I have two characters locked in a war of words waiting for me."

The politician laughed. "I have *a* ticket tomorrow; I'll be rooting for you."

"Thanks for your support." Urban returned to his typewriter. After the talk they had had in the copy room she was avoiding bringing up something with Matt that was really bothering her. Now the politician was betwixt and between.

Click.

VI

On the bench in front of the fire station Mathew Jason Benson sat waiting with his brown bag sipping his diet cola. He watched a beautiful sight pull up in a Volkswagen and park across the street in the parking lot of a gas station. Justine Anabeth Duchane did look both ways and diagonally cross the street carrying her own paper bag.

"Hey there." The big EMT grinned, he was in uniform.

"Hey yourself." She sat next to him in her beige conservative ankle length dress and matching flats.

The politician pulled out tuna on rye and a Tab. Her date pulled out baloney on a hard roll. They clinked cans.

"Jeremy gave me the results." She waited. "I passed."

"Matt, that's awesome." She kissed him. Fast track to promotion for her boyfriend.

"Good thing I'm a sucker for a man in uniform because you always will be."

Benson grinned at his girlfriend. "Well, I'm sucker for a girl with a master's degree." They both took a bite of lunch.

"You guys expected a full plate tonight?" He shook his head.

I hope not," Duchane sipped her soda.

"I'm going to Hal's play again tonight, tonights the night the big wigs from all over New England will be there. This one matters the most." That was true.

This could make a career for him. It could also send him back to drawing board with six month's salary to figure it out.

"I'll stop and light a candle," Matt half joked. "I hope he gets it."

"So let's talk about us. Something's been bothering you the last week or two," Justine spoke calmly. "We haven't made love in weeks." The EMT dropped his sandwich in the bag and rubbed his face.

"I...I wanted to put this off until after the election..." *Did his voice just crack*? Justine waited but he was not forthcoming. She also replaced her sandwich and reached for his hand. He let her take and that was a good sign. Duchane studied Benson's eyes. "I... think it's time to talk about a big step, but you have enough on your plate. I'm going to be there all day for two days making calls for you to get those votes. I was going to bring things up after." He looked embarrassed and ready to cry.

"Whatever it is, you can tell me." He put his drink down and took her other hand.

"I'm a thirty-two year-old gainfully employed man. I don't sport screw. I've been looking for a wife and you are right for the job. I love you... I think we should get engaged, after the election, so it doesn't affect your campaign."

"Oh my God Matt. That's wonderful. Of course I'll marry you." Justine kissed him. "After the election." They grinned. "That was it?"

"Yeah." They leaned back and sighed.

"Phew."

VII

Ralph, the thespian who was playing the antihero on the Cannonville Playhouse was brilliant. The whole show went off without a hitch. "Author Author! Was begun somewhere in the back of the auditorium, possibly by a chestnut haired politician. Horatio Albert Urban got a standing ovation. The writer had arrived.

After what felt like a billion handshakes and even a begrudging "congratulations" from Coyt, the actors left, the audience left, the well-wishers left and prospective producers left. More than two hours after the play was over a stagehand put the light on the front center of the darkened stage for the ghosts--yes theater people are that superstitious and the remaining stagehands were cleaning the wings and the lobby.

Hal sat next to that light feeling very numb. *Why don't I feel great?* He was on the verge of every dream he ever had.

Someone opened a door at the back of the theater and a stagehand gestured to him and was thanked. A figure walked down the aisle to him in the darkness. "Hey stranger," it was Justine. She hopped up on the stage next to him using both hands to swing up. They sat next to each other, legs hanging down.

"What's new?" Oh there was loads, but this was his night, Duchane tried to hold in her news. It wasn't easy.

"Isn't your leading man a bit...perfect." They laughed. "I thought you said he was too young?" Fair question.

"Makeup and talent go along away," Urban explained.

"Oh," she chuckled. "I get it." They sat there in silence. There were noises from the green room, stagehands cleaning and setting up for the Saturday matinee. The Green Room was like they were all over the theater world, not green. Old couches and chairs in a mostly circle, some naugahyde, some not. There were some old desks and tables, probably because it doubled as second prop room and a few makeup tables in the corners.

"The show was great."

"Thank you." He sounded flat, Hal had said that too many times that evening.

"Let's go up the street. I'm buying you dinner at Cannonville Diner to celebrate," Justine ordered and hopped down.

"Um, okay." He hopped down. "Thank *you*."

"We can discuss the campaign too, if you like." That always perked him up. She knew him, well, mostly. Sometimes we're blind.

"As you wish." They walked up the aisle and through the outer room. A blonde stagehand, all in black, was vacuuming.

Outside Duchane looked at the sky. "I had some good news tonight as well," she couldn't hold it in anymore.

"I could use some good news." Hal grinned and his friend unlocked the car.

"Matt wants to get engaged after the election." That wasn't quite what he meant. *No!* Urban was hurt. Why?

The writer leaned on top of the car and looked across the roof at his friend. "That's great. I want you to be happy." Of course he wanted her to be happy. That's what Matt was good for.

"I am." Her eyes were dancing. That was good news. Horatio Albert Urban smiled his best, most convincing smile. It even fooled his best friend.

They had been dead inside when they met and now things were on the up and up. Driving up US-1 Urban asked a question. "Where's the ring?"

"He doesn't want it to affect the election. he'll get it after." Duchane was a giggly as a teenager now. Benson was wise.

"Can't fault him there." The writer was watching storefronts.

"So, tell me the truth, do you think other playhouses want you? How do *you* think it went?" The writer gave the politician his best smile again. Maybe he should try acting.

"Oh I am so in." They high fived.

THE ELECTION

Friday night before the election. The play had been a success and Horatio Albert Urban had his run. Of course that was weeks away, he had a break. Tonight Booker had a date, Sam had a date and, of course, Justine and Matt were on a date. The writer needed a real break. He drove down River Street to

Pennyless Video. Ellis Bennett, Liz's sister, me if you remember, worked there. I was also on a date with whatever boyfriend I had that week.

So I wasn't there. My enigmatic employer, Richard Blaine Doyle, was running it that evening. Well, the sandy haired Vietnam veteran sat, leaning back in his grey chair, with his work boots on the counter, dress shirt untucked and wearing tight jeans watching John Wayne on the four tvs on display in the video store. There was a wartime scar on his cheek. We had every title imaginable and only he owned it to stay sane, he was a private investigator. Of course Doyle barely looked up when customers walked in.

The store had several open air racks of white wire shelves around the room. "Let me know if you need help," my employer couldn't have sounded less interested.

"Don't want what you can't have," the writer mumbled.

"Under E, in classics, *Enchantment* with David Niven, old lonely man who never got the woman he loves." Still the owner did not look up but he did scratch his scar.

Urban walked up the raised counter that Doyle used for privacy and spoke. "I'm Hal."

"Horatio Albert Urban," still the detective didn't look up. "You've been a member seven years, rent about once every three months, almost always late and have never failed to pay a fine." The writer looked at the TV and back at the owner confused.

"Guilty," he put his hands out palms up.

"It pays to know my customers," the proprietor yawned. "Newspaper says you are one hell of a playwright. Maybe I'll have one of them on video someday."

"Well, I prefer the stage." Barely noticing him, and not looking up, Doyle shrugged.

"At least you're more honest than your uncle." The big veteran sighed.

"You know Uncle Hal?" Urban had been named for his uncle, the first selectman and they kept the relationship secret.

"I've...encountered him. No one can blame you because he's a crook and liar." *So how do you really feel?*

"Um, thanks, I guess." What was he going to say?

"Ellis says that Liz conned her into helping you get your friend elected to town council." Something in the veteran's eyes changed and he did look at the writer.

Now the detective was paying attention. "We went to high school together, Ellis and I."

"I know. I also see the problem. Your friend Justine. Forget about her. Love doesn't always feel good." *He got all that from my face? Shit!* "Sometimes you just need to cut your losses." Doyle went back to his movie.

"How can you say that?" Hal was dejected, my boss just waved his hand without looking up. No one was a threat to the proprietor.

"Stay friends, don't stay friends, that's up to you. But you're clearly in love with her and it's like you said," the cold eyes of the veteran looked through the writer's eyes into his soul. "Don't want what you can't have." He went back to the movie, again.

"How do you know all this?" My boss chuckled.

"It's all over your face and she's not here." The Duke said something witty and the detective chuckled.

"Wow, if I ever need a detective I know who to ask." Just a shrug.

"Where is she tonight?" He knew the answer though.

"On a date." Doyle looked at him again.

"Well, that it's it, isn't it? You're her *friend*. Now, you can keep agonizing over it or let her go." He looked back at John Wayne. "So, you want that movie or not?"

"You ever love someone like that?" The detective got up and stood his full six one and one half. Urban thought he was dead. Doyle looked at the counter under the front window and then turned to look out the side window near him.

"This is not about me bud." He stared up River Street.

"So that's a yes." Doyle turned to Hal.

You've worked her campaign, got her to a seventy percent promise rate that she'll get elected?" Hal nodded. "Probably on the phone all the time?" Nod. "And she's still out with someone else?"

"Yeah."

"So's mine." That's all my employer would say about that. "You want that movie or not?" Urban walked to the exit.

"Maybe an action movie instead?" The owner chuckled.

"I have *Lethal Weapon* right here." Hal smiled.

"Good choice." He paid the two dollars. "Thank you, sir."

"No stripes on my sleeve." Then he turned and went back to his movie before the writer even left.

"Night," Doyle barely waved a hand.

Horatio Albert Urban got back in his car and drove away. There was something rotten in the state of Connecticut. *Alas poor Horatio. You should've made up your mind.*

Old soldiers are wise.

Is this the end?

"How am I supposed to do this Justine?" Hal asked the nobody in his car. "I am such a hypocrite." When did this start? When had his feelings become...this?

He had dreamed of becoming a writer.

It had come true.

It was straw.

She made him better.

He was making her a champion.

She wanted a good man and dreamed of a political career.

She had both.

Why couldn't he be happy for her?

Were they just friends, Hal and Justine?

He had to let her go.

After the election.

VIII

'A special table,' had been the request that the proprietor had gotten. So a table in the back had been prepared. The co-owner of Luigi's was a hopeless romantic.

"Make sure they get the best treatment," he ordered a dark haired Rumanian waiter named Mike.

"Yes sir." The younger man was a good waiter.

"She will be my councilwoman tomorrow," it was a late dinner, no calls after 8pm. The waiter was cleaning a table and Tony went to great customers.

Two doors down was Sarah's Fine Jewelry Shop and Benson was with Duchane picking out a ring. "Do you want a theme ring?"

"Not at all." She grinned, looking at white gold and small stones. "I could even live without a diamond." Justine was a simple girl.

"Nothing of that," the EMT was following her gaze. "Only the best for you and that one is a bit small."

"So is my appetite for the glamorous," the politician giggled.

"I understand." Benson looked up the owner, a brown haired cougar with glasses and a low cut grey sweater.

"May I see that one," he pointed to a medium sized stone with simple band.

"Of course," she got it of the case and the prospective bride examined it. "Beautiful choice, though I will need to size it down."

"Nah," Justine crinkled her nose, "too big, how about that one."

"Alright," the older woman switched rings. "How's that?" The couple looked at each other. "I have some…"

"I love it," Duchane argued. "With this, I'm easy." I know that's a first. or maybe it just didn't sound right.

"She's the boss." Benson grinned.

"May I size your finger?" Sarah put the ring out of reach and got a ring of aluminum rings. One would slip perfectly on the politician's finger.

"Of course." The politician held her hand out. "Matt, it's perfect."

"You're perfect." He kissed her. The jeweler took notes. She had heard the mushy stuff all before.

"Is Wednesday alright?" She asked.

The couple looked at each other. "Perfect," Justine spoke up.

"Ten percent down and the balance at pick up." The EMT got his credit card out. He was beaming. This was not new for Duchane, but he was a better man than Kurt.

"Thank yous," were exchanged after a signature and receipt were exchanged.

Outside the politician spoke, "I like the store."

"She went to high school with my dad," Matt explained. Then he opened the door to Luigi's. *Does my fiancé know everybody in town?*

"Convenient too." There was Tony as frenetic as ever.

"Matthew, Justine, so good to see you." He rushed to them and took her hand in his, kissing it. Then he pumped Benson's.

"Good to see you," Duchane pecked the older man on the cheek.

"Thank you." He beamed.

"Hey Tony." The EMT was not a poet.

"Please come with me," he waved to bartender who bent down to open the bar fridge to get the chilled alcohol. "I am so confident in this young lady; champagne is on the house."

"You don't have to do that," the politician argued, "it could be construed as a bribe." Alone in the crowd the three of them laughed.

"Well, then it's a promotion gift for Matthew," Tony recovered fast. "Congratulations."

"I haven't filled an opening yet," they turned left in the back room to the special table. "Just passed a test."

"With your work ethic, it's just a matter of time," the older man argued. "Please sit. Mike will be taking care of you."

The Rumanian brought waters. "Excuse me."

"Like Patton, I shall return," the owner spoke up and walked away. *Wasn't Patton…*

The bartender brought the champagne, in a bucket and two glasses. "Matt."

"Cap," He served. "Hey Mike."

"Do you need any other drinks?" The waiter asked.

"Nah," they looked at each other. "Two prime rib…" Justine ordered. They always had the same order at Luigi's place.

"Thank you." The waiter and the bartender left. They clinked glasses.

"You are the kind of guy that girls dream about Matthew Jason Benson." The soon to be fiancé looked starry eyed.

"Um thank you." He put the glass down. "I try to be a good boyfriend." He took her hand. "And you make it easy even when you're OCD."

She giggled. "OCD ain't bad."

"Nah." They laughed. "We can talk dates after the election."

"Well, I'm not campaigning right now. What were *you* thinking?" Why was she putting it all on him?

"Saint's M's," basilica, his church, "has a six month waiting period that would put us in May or June."

"We could call them Wednesday," Justine rubbed his hand.

"That was my thought." Benson agreed. It was like they were alone in a room full of people. They didn't even notice when their salads were served.

"May I try it out?" He shrugged, not sure what she meant.

"You may." What was she thinking?

"Ahem," the politician cleared her throat. "Justine Anabeth Benson." That was a different sound. The couple smiled at it.

"I like it," Matt really did.

"It'll do," Duchane joked and they laughed. They stared in each other's eyes for a while quietly. They were lost in the good way.

"Are you worried about tomorrow?" Benson asked, changing the subject.

"I'm," the politician squeezed his hand tighter, "no, no I'm not. Win or lose it is not my last election and I will be a successful politician."

"What comes next?" He was befuddled. Hal always said *'issues first and the rest will follow, like your column.'*

"Well, state rep, most likely, unless by some reason the democrats shit the bed with the first selectman's chair." *Hal Opus, though a crook, is really popular*. Amazing how those two Hals came from the same gene pool.

"And if it all goes well?" The EMT was learning, the more she told him the better chance he had at remembering. He would a politician's hubby after all.

"By forty state senate and by fifty, governor, that's my dream," Justine had had to tell him all this before but at that moment she didn't care.

"Governor Benson?" Their eyebrows went up. She'd hadn't thought about that.

"Yes I suppose it would be." They were laughing when their salads were removed and waters refilled.

"Isn't that a sitcom?" The EMT asked.

"Well, he was the governor's butler." The politician laughed. "Give me *Star Trek* any day."

"Hey, then I have to call this off, Red Shirt." They laughed.

"I'm not a red shirt, I'd be the captain. Captain Duchane." Yup, she was an alpha.

IX

Early in the morning the Office of the Registrar of Voters counted the absentee ballots in Cannonville. That had been another pet project for Urban. In the only district that you, dear reader, care about of the nine candidates, three republicans, three unaffiliated and three democrats, all the republicans and one democrat had won town council seats. Justine Duchane led those returns by leaps and bounds.

For those in the know that is good shot in the arm for any campaign as usually absentees are a good microcosm for any election. Hal woke Justine up with repeated use of the doorbell. That one always worked. No matter how his feelings had played out, Horatio Albert Urban had promised an election and she was going to win.

The writer was overflowing with coffees and donuts as well as bagels and scones. He was in jeans and a Rose Thorns hoody. Justine wore her old sweats. "Oh my God, I created a monster." That got him to grin.

"It's alive, it's alive," her friend joked at her bad hair morning. Matt and Book had to be on their way. Book was collecting Kelli. Matt was supposed to collect Pam.

"Really funny," Justine got out of his way and he brought all he was carrying to the kitchen table. They had installed four extra phone lines in the town home for her campaign. All out on this one. "That's for making this happen."

The candidate shut the door and went for a coffee. "I made you a promise and I'm keeping it," the writer assured his friend. "Take your coffee and go get in the shower. I'll get the voters lists ready."

"Thanks," Justine Anabeth Duchane retreated to her bathroom and turned the hot water on behind closed doors. This morning she even had to drink coffee in the shower. She felt young and it was as is her whole life was ahead of her. It was an exciting day. She had her boys and she had her political career.

Standing there the politician looked into the mirror. Full circle. Thirty sounded so old. It didn't feel old anymore. She had felt old on her thirtieth birthday and then Hal had rescued her and they had gone up to the festival. He had made her better.

It took longer to choose an outfit. She went with a teal Nancy Reagan pantsuit with her favorite flats. It seven when she joined the writer at the table with their voters lists.

"You did it Horatio Albert Urban," Hal didn't look up. "You made this happen."

"Seven months sober, an agent and twelve cities in twelve months," he grinned. "You made that happen." He got serious again.

There were lists spread around, pens and highlights ready. There was knock on the door and it opened. In walked Matthew Jason Benson alone. "Hi," he whispered and walked up to the list and phone that was waiting for him, but first the big EMT stooped to kiss his fiancé on the forehead. "You're going to win today."

All she did was look past him at the closed door. "Where's Pam?"

"I don't know," he picked up his campaign phone.

"I thought you were her ride?" Urban asked without looking up.

"She said she'd make her own way." Matt dialed his partner's number.

"Hell-oh," the voice came back very slowly on the other end.

"Did I wake you up?" Her partner asked, sitting down and taking a coffee. "Thank you," he mouthed. Mimicking the odd video store owner, Hal just waved. He was crossing out some names and highlighting others.

"Yes," the little EMT admitted, still half asleep.

"Are you still helping?" Benson asked, he also looked at the donuts and picked up a napkin. *Hmmm, Boston Crème.*

"Oh shit, yeah." There was a groan, a creek and a thud. "I may be a while."

"Like eleven?" He looked from Duchane to Urban, they were reading.

"Um, probably." How well he knew her. He knew what that really meant.

"Bring pizzas, we'll reimburse you when you get here." The campaign manager gave him a thumbs up.

"Okay." Tyler hung up.

"She'll be here by noon," the big man chuckled. There was another knock at the door.

"Come in Book," the candidate called.

In came Bertram Bryan Booker in his best silk suit and Kelli Jones in one of her favorite dresses. The phone rang. "Hello?" Justine answered it.

"We're about to go live," Dr. Elizabeth Victoria spoke cheerfully. Her husband was brewing coffee and I was snoring at their kitchen table. What are little sisters for?

"Thanks Doc," she told him. "Oh, Matt asked me to marry him," she was happy and she wanted to share it.

"That's beautiful, he's a lucky man." The doctor told her husband.

"I'm a lucky girl," Justine took Benson's hand. Hal didn't look up. "He's a perfect. Handsome, strong, sweet, romantic and thoughtful. He may not be a Harvard PhD but he can give me a run for my intellectual money and speaking of money he has a good job."

"Sounds like you have a checklist for him," Liz observed.

"Hal did actually, only the best for me," she eyed her friend, but he didn't look up. "It feels good Doctor."

"That's nice," Dr. Mark Burma took his wife's hand. "However, the important thing," the older woman looked in her husband's eyes, "when you're going through a courtship is to remember that a successful marriage is not about feelings."

"What about love?" The politician asked, confused.

"Oh we love each other," Liz kissed Mark. "But that's not why we got married and it's not why we stay married."

I woke up and rolled my eyes. "So what is?" Justine went on, still confused.

"A husband and wife need to complement each other. The purpose of a successful marriage is to make each other better. It's about growing as people," the attending physician went on. Mark nodded agreement.

"Thank you for the advice, I know I'm a better woman than I was seven months ago." For a split second Hal's eyes went up and then he went back to the voter's list.

"I hope that helps. We're going to start making calls for you now." The Burmas had three lines anyway, they were doctors. Also all of the campaign team could not fit in the small Duchane townhome. Town council campaigns don't rent offices.

"Thank you again." They hung up. Booker and Kelli were eating donuts and flipping through their voters lists. That whole day, in her apartment and the Burma home, call after call was made from the voters list. "Yes you agreed to vote Duchane, please remember to vote today," or a message to that effect.

There was a method to their madness. The campaign manager had researched, read harassed every successful candidate in the last ten years, even his asshole uncle--the first time Opus had spoken to his sister's 'idiot kid,' in ten years. The fact that *Nine Innings* had changed the first selectman's opinion of his nephew notwithstanding.

The fact was that in every election thousands of people in towns all over America who voice support for a candidate forget to vote. No one cared about town council anyway and even though the 1988 elections gave us another republican president, Cannonville was a liberal town. Hal had copied a scheme of getting voter commitments and then reminding them the weekend before and finally on the day.

"Why yes, I'm single," Booker was speaking into the phone with his velvety voice, "and yes if you remember to go to the polls and vote Duchane today you can win a date with me." That made Justine crinkle her nose. "Thank you. I will mark you as a yes and of course I'll be there." He hung up and looked up at the politician. "I don't even know where there is." She didn't laugh. he did.

"Hello, this is Justine Duchane," she spoke into the phone. "I'm your candidate for town council and I'm asking you for the good of the town to remember to vote for me today," she smiled. "That's great. Thank you."

"Hi this H. A. Urban of the SCREEK," he faked the sound of a phone garble, "committee, and we were just calling you today from headquarters to remind you to head down to the polls today and when you cast that vote for Bush, remember Justine Duchane, republican for town council." There was a pause. "Thank you."

"Hey, my name is Matt Benson. I'm one of your local EMTs. Someday I may save *your* life," he frowned, "no this is not a donation call. Thank you though. I'm calling to implore you to vote Duchane for town council."

"Hi. I'm Pam Tyler one of your local EMTs. Someday somebody you love is going to need me," click. "Hello, hello." She frowned. "Now that's just rude."

The two houses went on like that until seven.

There was an inbound call. "This is Burma household," I told Hal, "signing off."

"Thanks Ellis." He closed his voters list and tallied on his notepad.

"I hope she wins," and I hung up.

"Book Booker must head out," the heir to Billy Dee stood up and straightened his tie. "I have a date." What else was new? "Good luck, not that you need it." He also tossed Hal's hair on his way.

Justine ignored the empty pizza and donut boxes on the floor. "We have two hours. Urban looked at Kelli, Pam, Matt and Justine. "Let's call the nos."

"Hmm," Benson scratched his chin and looked at his fiancé.

The candidate smiled. "To the phones Robin."

At 9PM everyone's voices were hoarse and there would be no more calling. It had been a long day and it would be a surprise of epic proportions if she did not win. So the candidate put on the tea kettle and her campaign manager started to clean up.

"Night." Pam headed out.

"I have a date with Jack in OpEd. Good luck," Kelli Jones headed out and the three principals were alone.

"My boys," Justine Anabeth Duchane smiled ear to ear, "you were so helpful."

"Aw shucks," Matthew Jason Benson put on his best Jimmy Stewart.

"Promise kept," Horatio Albert Urban tossed a voter's list in the large trash can the campaign had bought. "Councilwoman Duchane." He smiled and went to the bathroom.

"You did it," Matt said when they were alone. Justine kissed him. "I love you."

"I love you too." They looked at the mess. He got to work and she turned on channel 12 news to get the results.

In the bathroom Hal finished and sat on the floor. It was the end. He began to cry. For the life of him the writer didn't know what else to do. He sat there for a long time and finally he cleaned his face and flushed the toilet. He washed his hands and sprayed some Lysol to give the illusion the delay had been biological and not emotionally.

In the living room The TV was just starting to give results. Urban helped Benson clean. "And we have a new town council woman in district two, with a new Cannonville record, eighty-nine percent of the voters for Justine Duchane,"--she actually squealed.

Then the councilwoman turned and threw her arms around Hal. "Thank you." He hugged her back. He was saying goodbye.

"I knew you'd win." They separated and then she turned to Matt, giving him a lover's embrace. They kissed. The writer kept cleaning.

"Congratulations love." They also separated.

After all the results had been announced and most of the cleaning done the EMT absented himself to the bathroom. "Hal what do you say you take one handle and I take the other?"

Looking exhausted and numb, he nodded. "Okay." They picked up the can and went out the front door.

"What happens tomorrow playwright?" Duchane asked.

"Tomorrow it's meetings in New Haven." He shut the door and they walked along the outside of the rows of homes to the dumpster.

"You're a success Mister Urban." He shrugged.

"*Councilwoman* Duchane." His car was closer to the dumpster than the door and he had left it unlocked. It was an old rusty white Chevy. That had been the closest open space.

Justine tied the bag. "Together?" He nodded. What couldn't they accomplish together?

They tipped the can into the dumpster and put it down. He let go and stretched, taking a step away. "This friendship has to end Justine," it sounded so final.

"Hal, what are you talking about? You're my *best* friend. I'm a better person because of you." At y-o-u the councilwoman almost hesitated.

"And I'm a lot better person because of you. But this," he gestured between them, "isn't friendship. This," he gestured again, "is something more. You are the love of my life. I don't know why; I don't know when. But you have," Urban pointed to her townhome, "the love of your life. You don't need me anymore."

And how he needed her. "What do you mean Hal? Of course I need you." Duchane was in shock. She just stood there, shaking.

"I can't be a third wheel; it's--hell you deserve so much better than me." The writer opened his car door.

"What do you mean?" She took a step and he fished for his keys.

"I love you Justine but I'm not good enough for you. You deserve to spend the rest of your life with a better man than me...and I deserve better than watching the woman I love with someone else--

hearing the play by play, even if he's the right guy and I'm not."

"The right guy?" Now Duchane was crying and Urban was fighting not to.

"I love you too much to fight for you. I want you to be with the man who makes you feel good." *Feel good?* "I can't just be friends with you. We had a deal and we both kept to it. Good bye Justine." The writer shut the door and peeled out of the parking.

That is when he started to cry.

The politician trudged back to her front door, forgetting the garbage can. The big EMT stood in the doorway. "Matt?"

"Hey baby," he saw her crying and then she buried her head in his chest. "It's okay. I'm here. What's wrong?"

Epilogue

Final dress rehearsal at Hartfield Theater for *Nine Innings'* New Year's Eve weekend opening. The second of twelve theaters in twelve months. Five grand a theater and an agent negotiating a three play deal. Hal had arrived and once his play saw the light of day he'd done it on his own. He now had the most in prestigious weekend in any Connecticut Theater. The only places higher would be off or on Broadway.

The writer sat in the front row with a copy of his play and clipboard taking notes for the actors. "No, no, no." The director, a muscular woman with short blonde hair and off color loose trousers and sweater jumped up. She also wore an artsy scarf. "That's not what I want." She bounded onto the stage.

"I caught your play in New Haven," a voice came from behind Hal. He turned.

There was a wealthy looking man in a black three-piece suit that matched his hair standing behind him. "I assume there's a second half to that sentence?" Urban asked.

"Yes. There is. I also read the review that called you the next Neil Simon," the stranger went on. They spoke in hushed voices as the director yelled at actors on stage.

"Flattering," was all the writer could think to say.

"I'm Monte Norman," now that was a big deal. Seven time Tony nominated producer--though he had yet to win one.

"Now this is an honor," Horatio Albert Urban stood up. He dropped his play and clipboard and shook the tall man's hand.

"Any more Jewish heritage plays in that brain of yours?" Actually two of the three plays his agent was shopping were also based on his maternal family of origin.

"Yes," it was a confused and astonished affirmative.

"Do you have an agent?" Monte was fishing in his breast pocket. All Urban could do was nod. "Take my card. You two show me them. I think I may have a job for you this coming summer." Urban put the card in his pocket.

"Wow." Norman chuckled.

"Close your mouth Hal." He did. "I haven't read them yet." Smirking, the producer walked away. All the writer could do was watch.

"Mr. Urban?" A stagehand, about nineteen, blonde, skinny and in all black was approaching him.

"Hey Chelsea," he didn't look at her.

"I have a package for you." She held up a little black box. The kind a ring is sold in. "You have a friend into *Lord of the Rings* or something?"

Horatio Albert Urban took the box. There was a piece of paper folded up inside. "Oh boy." He opened it.

"What's that?" The stagehand asked. But the playwright was shaking. He read the paper. *Holy shit.*

'How does July 15th sound?'

"Oh my--is the woman still here?" Urban looked at Chelsea.

"She out by the box office," but before the word 'box,' the writer was sprinting.

There she was. Justine Anabeth Duchane stood in a long tan coat over blue jeans, sneakers and warm green turtleneck sweater. Her hands had no jewelry.

"Where's...?" Urban's voice cracked. "What?"

"Is that all you can say Hal?" the councilwoman asked. "It's been a long lonely six weeks and I know I've had trouble sleeping without my last call."

"What about Matt?" In response she reached up and pulled on the neck of her sweater. There was no jewelry. "I don't understand."

"I may have *wanted* that necklace, but I *needed* something better. That was true but he was slow on the uptake.

You're the future governor of Connecticut, you deserve a husband with broad shoulders, strong chin, romantic heart and stable job." Hal really had none of those. "You want to spend your life with Matt. I'm a drunk for God's sakes."

"Are you sober?" She was concerned.

"Very." Ever since the alley.

"Good. Now listen carefully. You don't get to choose who I spend the rest of my life Horatio Albert Urban," she was fighting mad. She was fighting for him. "You said you love me."

"You said that was different than the way Matt did." That was true.

Maybe. However, what is love good for if it's not to make each us the best us we can be? You and I are so much better together. We're a team." Horatio Albert Urban took a step forward.

"I don't know anymore." Had he become jaded this winter?

"Could you have accomplished this?" She pointed to the marquee with his name one it, "last March?"

"No," was his sheepish response. The doors to the auditorium cracked open. Stagehands, actors and even the director were peeking out with baited breath.

"Could I have been elected to town council? Would I have come so far so fast? Could either one of us have opened up to anyone?" The writer tried to answer but his voice cracked. "Would you have quit drinking? Would you have campaigned for me? Would I have cared enough to proof your plays for typos? I am a much better person than before we went to the festival," now Justine took a step forward. they were meeting in the middle of the room.

"So am I." Hal took another step.

"You made me this way." Justine took another, "this is the kind of husband I need. Someone that makes me better. Someone I make better." They were almost close enough. "*You're* the man I plan to spend the rest of my life with Hal Urban."

"Oh what the hell," the box and note were dropped and they were in a passionate embrace. That made the whole company applaud. "Uh," our heroes looked at the now open doors. Duchane giggled.

"See, everything you write is a hit." Urban chuckled.

"I think you wrote this one." He kissed her again.

fin